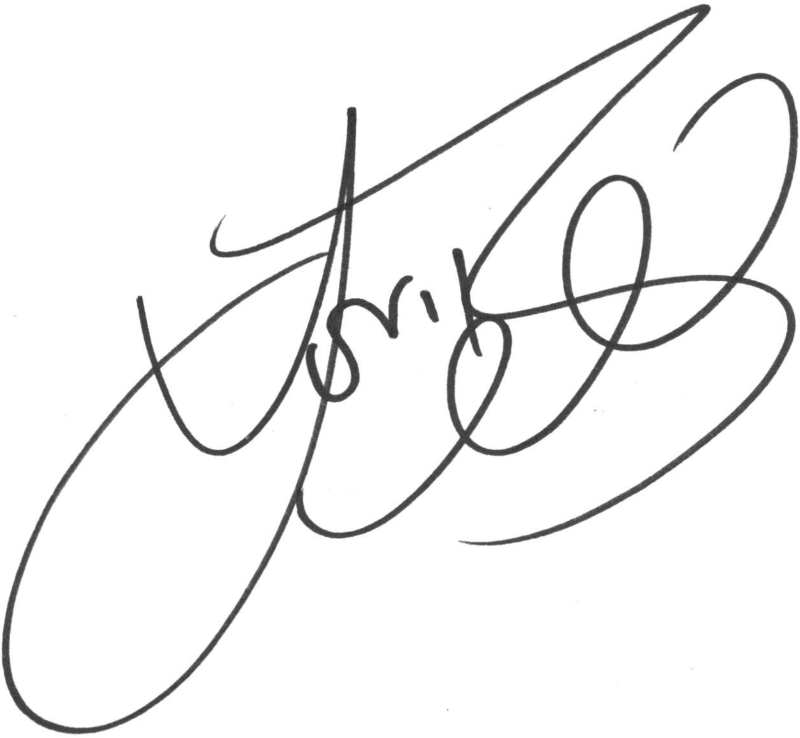

If Things Were Different

Lori Bell

This book is a work of fiction. Names, characters, places and incidents are the product of the author's imagination or are used fictitiously. Any resemblance to actual events, locales, or persons, living or dead, is coincidental.

Copyright © 2018 by Lori Bell

All rights reserved. This book or any portion thereof may not be reproduced or used in any manner whatsoever without the express written permission of the publisher except for the use of brief quotations in a book review.

Cover photograph by CanStock Photo

Printed by CreateSpace

ISBN 978 1721863518

DEDICATION

To my readers, loyal from the very beginning, and brand new.
My life would be so different and much less fulfilling if I could not create story after story for all of you.

1

"If things were different, of course I'd be ahead of schedule at this point," Nash Parker spoke to their party of four, seated at a small square table tucked in the corner of a crowded Mexican restaurant. All Saylor Bach heard him say was *if things were different*. The rest of his words she had drowned out with her thoughts.

In a flash, she was back there again with him. Two decades ago when they were both nineteen. Young. Carefree. Dreamers. They were merely kids, really, harboring adult feelings. But at the time they were truly in love.

His light brown hair was somewhat shorter now. His bangs no longer swept over his blue eyes. There was still some length. His hair was hardly short cropped. And it wasn't thinning or graying for a man of almost forty. He easily captured the image of carefree, or perhaps rebellious. Not quite a bad boy, then or now. But Nash always had just enough defiance to keep him veered off the straight and narrow path. That made Saylor smile inside. She would giggle aloud at the thought right now if she were alone. Instead, she was in the company of Nash and his wife, Londyn. And her own husband, Max.

Saylor took a long sip of her margarita, which she preferred sans the salt around the rim of the glass. The alcohol made her feel sentimental and delved her deeper into her thoughts, and further down a path full of the memories she held onto.

She caught herself twisting the narrow, braided, gold ring she wore on her pinky finger. Max had spoken something to her. "Honey? You're worlds away. What are you thinking about?" Apparently someone had asked her a direct question in this group conversation and she had been oblivious to it.

"Oh, sorry," Saylor paused, and her face flushed. She couldn't say what, *or who,* was on her mind.

"I'm headed to the little girl's room. Join me?" Londyn asked her, for what must have been the second time. They weren't terribly close in the bonded girlfriend sense. Londyn was entirely more open with her than Saylor cared to be in return. They certainly weren't the type of girlfriends who went to the restroom together in pairs.

If Things Were Different

"I think I'll stay here and finish this," Saylor raised her glass, and Londyn left their table. She had long dark hair in contrast to Saylor's timeless platinum blonde bob. She had a side part with side swept bangs that gave her hairstyle a soft appearance as it often lay on her jawbone when she didn't have it tucked behind one or both ears. Saylor looked chic. Londyn was all lady. She had never-ending, slender legs that practically reached up to her neck, as opposed to Saylor's shorter, muscular limbs. Her skin tone was porcelain, while Saylor's was tanned. She loved the sun. The black, sleeveless, ruffled shift dress that she wore accented her suntan, even inside a dimly lit restaurant.

"I'll go pay the bill," Max offered. The couples took turns treating the other to occasional nights out, and tonight's dinner was courtesy of Max and Saylor.

For a moment, while they were alone at the table, Nash only stared at her. She felt his eyes on her, so she in turn kept her head down and focused on her glass. He watched her trace the water droplets trickling down the exterior with her fingertips. This wasn't the first time he had noticed her pinky ring. Never had there been an appropriate moment to mention it though. He also knew some things were better left unsaid. But he didn't care about knowing better. He never did. She had loved that about him once.

"You've worn that ring in some way since I gave it to you." Nash remembered a time when she was pregnant and he had spotted it on a simple gold chain around her neck. Her hands had been too swollen to wear any rings on her fingers then.

She looked up. She made eye contact with him before she spoke in answer. "You've noticed?"

"You know I have," he said. "I like knowing it still means something to you after all these years." He wanted to believe that *he* still meant something to her as well. But what did it matter? They both had moved on. They were committed to other people. Their lives were separate, yet still intertwined. That was both a blessing and a curse.

Saylor nodded before she smiled at him. "I'm a little tipsy, so I had better use caution with what I say," she giggled. The way she threw her head back when she laughed at her own silliness sent a familiar feeling reeling through his mind, body, and soul that had never perished.

"Oh what the hell," he chuckled. "It's only me."

"Yeah, it's only you," she said cautiously in response, before his wife now returned to their table. And yes, for Saylor, it had always been only him. *Only Nash.*

Londyn looked as if she had reapplied her makeup. It was obvious her deep plum lipstick was fresh. She let her short coral skirt ride up her thighs a bit after she sat down corner to corner to both her husband and Saylor. Londyn knew of their past, *of course she knew,* but never appeared to think anything of it. Funny remarks here and there over the years, in reference to their once-upon-a-time relationship which was now history, had pretty much assured Saylor that Londyn did not feel threatened. *And she shouldn't,* Saylor thought. *There was nothing left between her and Nash but memories.* Some women though were insecure about their men and former flames. Saylor felt it was a

If Things Were Different

sure bet that Londyn never lacked confidence about anything in her life. She was beautiful. Her skin was flawless, her body was shapely in all the right places. And again, those legs were endless. In heels, she was eye level with Nash's six-one frame. Saylor didn't necessarily envy Londyn for her height. She didn't want to be that dang tall. She just would have liked to have topped off at five-five or five-six, instead of barely five-three. Her body had curves though. She was blessed with a sexy figure, and Saylor worked hard to keep it that way. At nearly forty years old, she had heard things could begin to drop and sag overnight. Father Time was known not to show much mercy.

"I saw Max paying the bill, and chatting it up with the owner," Londyn stated, as if to explain why she made it back to the table before him, and Saylor noticed a perfectly white front tooth of hers had been marked by a deep plum lipstick stain. She kept silent. They weren't close enough girlfriends to cease awkward things like food on your face, an eyelash on your cheek, or makeup mishaps. And besides, the temporary imperfection amused her. "Thank you again for dinner."

"No thanks necessary. Tag you're it, next time." Saylor's comment drew a laugh from them at the table just as Max returned and they began to scoot back their chairs and stand up. Max wore flat front khaki chinos and a fitted long-sleeve white button down shirt. He looked handsome, but Saylor had thought he should have worn a shirt with color, or solid black. She especially liked when he wore a black shirt as it complimented his coal black hair. He didn't have a sporadic grey hair on his head — yet. Nash was wearing dark denim with a powder blue button down. The blue shirt made his eyes pop. As if Saylor needed any additional help looking into those eyes. She painfully strived to avoid doing just that. It was always more difficult when she had been drinking to not let herself go there, *to fall back into her solemn thoughts of what might have been, if things had turned out differently.* Alcohol brought out her vulnerability with him. *Damn the tequila tonight.*

Saylor stepped away from the table, following Max. He had not thought to be polite, nor gentleman-like, to wait and allow her to walk in front of him first. She all but rolled her eyes at him, and then she watched Nash place his hand on the small of Londyn's back as they too moved away from the table. Nash stopped after two strides forward, and he looked back at Saylor. "You coming?"

She nodded, and took a couple quick steps in her black, low heeled, strappy sandals to catch up to all of them. He smiled at her. One of those pure, sweet smiles that lit up his eyes. And her insides flip flopped.

It was time to go home and sober up. And return to reality.

2

Saylor felt the same sense of welcome from the quirky charm of their cottage on the beach in Morehead City, North Carolina every single time she walked the narrow cobblestone sidewalk up to their home. Surfboards were almost always propped from the ground up and against the columns that supported the overhang of the front porch. Saylor had given those narrow-width, square columns a fresh coat of white paint last spring, but fractions were peeling away again. That was part of the cottage's appeal. It was rustic and lived in. The radish red siding was a simple contrast with the white columns and floorboards on the front porch. She had also painted two of the wooden high-back rocking chairs out there a shade of pale yellow. This was her home on the beach, and it had been for the past fifteen years of her life. She and Max had raised their baby boy there throughout every single one of those years, and then just five years ago, along came a second child that they had all but given up on having. A baby girl had finally and so perfectly completed their family of four then.

Sammy was fifteen, and Syd was a decade younger. The two of them were Saylor's whole world, and she shouldn't have had to, but she reminded herself of that fact tonight — after allowing herself to question if things were different. *What if she had chosen a life with Nash?* Well, for one, she would not have her two beautiful children.

Little Syd was asleep on one end of the sofa, her body curled up to make her look even smaller, when they walked into the cottage. And on the opposite side, Sammy was awake and lounging with his bare feet propped up on the glass-topped wagon wheel coffee table. He looked up at them and then back at the movie he was watching on the TV that Saylor thought was playing entirely too loud. Max never hesitated to take on the role of a loving daddy, as Saylor watched him and smiled, when he carefully scooped up their sleeping daughter into his arms and carried her down the hallway to her bedroom.

Saylor plopped down beside her son on the sofa. Their shoulders touched. Saylor's arms were bare in her dress, and Sammy's were covered by the white short-sleeved David Bowe t-shirt that he wore with long, frayed khaki cargo shorts. She nudged him to take his attention away from the movie. "Thanks for taking such good care of your baby sis," she said to him. He grinned and held out his hand, open palm, insinuating that she owed him some money. Saylor giggled. "Your payment is propped against the pillar out front. You're going to work for that board this summer." The brand new surfboard outside, adjacent to his father's old and battered *lucky* one, was her teenage son's current greatest treasure. He had begged for it, and sworn he would do absolutely anything the entire summer if he could have it — even babysit his little sister.

If Things Were Different

"I'm going out first thing in the morning." He meant surfing, and Saylor had expected nothing less. He was always on the water. "You are your father's son," she told him, as she kicked off her sandals and propped her bare feet up on the table next to his. His feet were already huge, especially in comparison to hers. He was sprouting too fast. His facial features were changing, he was pimpled faced, and a little awkward at times. His growth spurts and maturity level weren't exactly parallel. He was beginning to look like a man, yet he still acted very much like a boy. Sammy's dark hair swept above one eye as he turned his head and grinned. He didn't mind being compared to his father. He adored him. He was the man who taught him all about the love of surfing. Sammy's adoration for that water sport knew no bounds. It was all he cared about, other than his family, on most days. He was a wave rider. He was a natural on the deep face, or forward, of a moving wave. He rarely flubbed. His balance on that board was impeccable almost every single time he was carried to shore. His father taught him the tricks and trade to it all. And his mother understood his profound need to be out there on the water.

When the movie ended, Sammy stood up and announced he was going to bed. "Night, night," Saylor spoke to him, as she pressed two fingers to her lips and blew him a kiss. Sammy smirked and waved off her sentimentality as he too made his way down the hallway in their cottage.

After turning down the volume on the television, while the closing credits to the movie rolled, she sat back and pressed her head against the sofa cushions behind her. She tugged at her short black dress, partially covering the tops of her tanned thighs. She wondered if Max went to bed without telling her goodnight. She thought of Nash and Londyn at the restaurant tonight. As always, they seemed happy and content together. Sometimes she was grateful for how their lives were still intertwined. She would not have liked not knowing where Nash ended up. Or with whom. Sometimes though she wondered if she was better off not knowing. Because then, she wouldn't have to over think it. Like tonight.

She intended to only momentarily close her eyes as she sat there with her head back. She didn't plan to fall asleep and dream about how her life once was.

*

Londyn closed the front door of the elaborate four-bedroom, four-bath condominium that she lived in with Nash and now infrequently their nineteen-year-old daughter, who was living away from home and experiencing her first year of college life.

She stood inside the entrance of her home, with her back up against the door. She slipped off her heels one by one. She heard herself sigh aloud. Drawn out and dramatic. *Was the evening really all that bad?* It was just another one of their typical dinners with conversations that utterly wore her out. She tried, and had given it her best effort for many years, to get Saylor Bach to like her, to be her friend. To accept her as Nash's wife, the mother of his only child. But no matter how big Saylor smiled, or the number of times she threw her head back in laughter, Londyn never saw her as genuine. At least not toward her. With Nash though, everything was authentic. The looks. The casual replies to anything he asked Saylor, whether it was something trivial or important. It exhausted Londyn. She kicked her shoes to the side, and padded barefoot on the wood flooring that led her to the open living room. She plopped down on the end of the white sofa, and curled her legs up underneath her. Then she heard Nash come in the front door. Out on the driveway, he had stayed in their car without explanation, and Londyn had gone ahead. He was always silent on the drive home after an evening out with them. Max Bach was his business partner, and one of his best friends. They saw each other daily, and at least quarterly they brought their wives into their circle for nights out, for dinner or cocktails. Londyn doubted there was business on his mind tonight. She always wondered if her husband thought of Saylor, especially once he spent time with her again. She didn't need a definite, honest, straightforward answer. Not when she already knew.

    Londyn's insecurities got the best of her from time to time, but she would never let it show. Because after all, she was Nash's wife. She was the mother of his child. She had what Saylor never would. Nash walked straight upstairs to their bedroom. And then Londyn got up from the sofa, flipped off the lights that were on, and followed him.

    He had already taken off his shirt, and stood in front of his dresser in only his denim, which were open at the fly. Londyn knew him well enough, his routine for everything, as she waited for him to take out a folded pair of boxers from the top, right-hand drawer, en route to the shower. His chest was tight and muscular, and already sunkissed.

"It was a fun night...with them...again." Londyn chose her words carefully. *Fun? It wasn't really.*

"It was," Nash was quick to agree. "Mexican food always seems to be a good choice. You know, everybody likes it." Londyn nodded. She cringed inside a little. She knew it was Saylor's favorite, and obviously her husband did too. "I should shower," he added, balling up his boxers in one of his large open-palmed hands.

"I might need some attention first..." Londyn spoke to him. Her voice was pure seduction. She unzipped the side of her short skirt and let it fall on the floor in front of him. She wore a black lacy thong underneath. She unbuttoned her blouse to reveal a matching black lacy bra. Her breasts spilled overtop of the cups. She had enhancements more than a decade ago. She wanted to ensure she kept a body that would turn her husband's head, even as they grew old together.

Nash looked at her for a moment, smiled, and shook his head while he chuckled. "Why does tequila always make you horny?" That wasn't the truth, but she played along. The truth was every single time they were in the company of Saylor, she felt a strong need to take her husband home and reclaim him as her own. And she tried to convince herself, always, after it happened, after the seduction, that their act wasn't overly passionate and intense because her husband was thinking of his former lover.

She pushed those thoughts out of her head and reached for him. She placed both of her hands inside the front of his open denim. It was quite obvious that he wasn't going to turn her down tonight. Nash took one hand and reached behind her

If Things Were Different

back to undo the clasp of her bra. He bent his head downward and found her nipples, one at a time, with is mouth. "You're beautiful," she heard him say to her, as she arched her back, and he braced her from behind with one of his arms. He dropped to his knees in front of her, and his teeth had ahold of the lace on her panties. She stood tall and she had gone from feeling powerless almost all evening to completely in control now. She enticed her husband to relish her body. He was attentive as he found her core, and when she came with urgency, she screamed out his name. She dropped to her knees in front of him then. He never kissed her, he never held her. She bent forward, on both her hands and knees now, and he rocked behind her, over and over again, until she exploded at her core once more. He expressed his pleasure with how he moved and moaned aloud in their big, empty condo. But the smile on Londyn's face slowly faded after she got what she wanted, because she couldn't help but think of how her husband had Saylor on his mind.

    Nearly two decades ago, Londyn and Nash shared a one night stand on the beach. They met at a party, where they had both been intoxicated for hours. They were attracted to each other, but from the moment she laid eyes on him, Londyn had fallen for him, body and soul. Their daughter was conceived that night in the sand. It was nearly nine months later before Londyn saw him again. Nash had been caught up in what she had hoped was a summer fling, but everyone she knew — who knew Nash and Saylor — had said they were passionately in love and already planning to spend the rest of their lives together. Londyn contemplated walking away then, as she had already kept their baby a secret from him. She wanted more for herself than to have a baby at nineteen years old. She had chosen to give birth, but pondered the possibility of giving up the baby for adoption. Nash would never have to know, and she could move on with her life. A life that still held so many possibilities as it was just beginning.

Londyn changed her mind though. And that was primarily because she loved Nash. She was young and selfish — and she wanted him. It really wasn't entirely about the baby. But Londyn would make it that way in Nash's eyes. He had a right to know that they conceived a child. She told him she was contemplating giving up the baby. She gave Nash Parker the freedom to walk away. But secretly, she counted on the fact that he was not that kind of man.

A solely sexual driven and alcohol enhanced one night stand on the beach, just weeks before he met Saylor, returned to haunt Nash and change the course of his life.

*

In the wee hours of the morning, Saylor opened her eyes from a dream. It was the same dream she always had. It was a rehash of reality. There were tears on her face now. Whether dreaming in her sleep, or just merely remembering at any sudden moment, Saylor always felt sadness rise in her chest and settle there. The pain hadn't really gone away. Saylor had just gotten used to it. She lived with it. Year after year.

If Things Were Different

She had never been more confident and sure of anything, or anyone, in her life back then. She and Nash were meant to spend their lives together. They clicked. They meshed. They liked — and disliked — all the same things. There, for a very short time, had been nothing in their way, nothing stopping them from taking on the world. That's how it felt when they were nineteen, naive, and in love.

And then there was the night that Saylor felt him pull away from her. It was abrupt and sudden. His shoulders were slumped and the look in his eyes was forlorn and lost. He had taken her for a walk in the moonlight on the beach. She carried her sandals, dangling from her fingers. And when they stopped walking, and he faced her, and he told her the truth that he had just discovered, her body went limp. Her fingers let go of the shoes that ended up in the sand. Her knees felt weak. Nash admitted he had no idea that he had gotten another woman pregnant. It happened before the two of them had met. She was a stranger. A one night stand. He had only known her first name. *But she was the mother of his child. He had to do right by her, for his child.* And if he married her, his parents would help them survive until they found jobs and were able to provide for their family. Suddenly, and so unfairly, Nash had a family. Without Saylor. There was no room for her in that equation. That's what he had essentially told her. But clearly, the choice to walk away from her, from them, was not one that he truly wanted to make.

They cried in each other's arms. They kissed and held on with intensity and defiance for what life had abruptly thrown at them. Just a few more seconds, another minute, another hour together. Goodbye had taken something from each of them many years ago. Their trust in true love was gone. Their faith in all good things coming to those who waited was tainted. Neither one of them had ever been in love before. But what was magical, and entirely too short-lived between them, had to come to an abrupt and heartbreaking end.

Saylor turned over, on her side, in bed next to her husband. Max was snoring lightly. She stared at his face. The face of the man who had saved her. He eased the pain of her heartache. She knew she couldn't have done it alone. She needed someone in order to move on with her life. Max had been there for her when his best friend betrayed her. The betrayal wasn't purposeful on Nash's end, but that one choice he made not only changed his life, but had broken Saylor's heart. And Max mended her heart the only way he knew how. By loving her with all of his being.

Saylor pulled the navy blue sheet away from her body, and moved out of their bed. Her active mind, jam packed with wonder and what ifs, kept her awake. She really wished sometimes that things had turned out differently. And she wasn't ashamed of those feelings — probably because she kept them to herself. *Everyone had secrets, or at least private thoughts that remained hidden.* Nash could have stayed committed to her, Saylor believed, while still providing for his child. He would have been a wonderful father either way. She assumed though, that he had grown to love Londyn. He stayed with her all these years, and together they raised a beautiful daughter. Saylor thought of her own children. The children Max gave her. Together they had created something special — a life. She loved him. She had just never been in love with Max the way she was with Nash. There was no fire in her soul when she said his name, or felt his touch, or looked into his eyes. It was a comfortable, safe kind of love. *And it was a good life*, Saylor reminded herself, as she stepped outside onto their front porch. The sky was completely dark. She sat out there on her yellow rocking chair infinite times during the nighttime hours. There was something both peaceful and lonely about being under the sky in the dark of night. It actually mirrored her life. Peaceful. And yet, lonely.

3

M&N Solar Energy Development was Max Bach's brainchild. Two decades prior, as a young man of barely twenty, he saw an opportunity to create his own business which focused on advancing technologies that used energy storage and provided the ability to generate predictable electricity when it's needed. There was a market for people and businesses who wanted to increase their use of green power. Max and Nash had grown up as friends. Nash knew well, all of Max's hopes and dreams to eventually supply and install solar power systems as a viable business. And when Max asked Nash to join forces with him to create and equally own M&N Solar Energy Development, Nash didn't hesitate. Max had given him no reason to. He had the financial backing from the bank to get his start. His plan was to supply and install solar power systems located on the roof or property of customers. There was a market out there for people who were motivated by the high costs of utility power. Max had thoroughly researched and well-educated himself on the topic. Nash was the people person, the salesman that Max sought to be fearless and persistent in business — just as Nash was in life. Nash was newly married with a brand new baby, so of course he agreed to partner up with Max. That partnership had paid off in spades as their business had flourished over the years in Morehead City and across the country.

If Things Were Different

After less than one year of being in business, both their friendship and partnership nearly fell apart. And it had everything to do with Saylor. Max wanted to pursue a relationship with his best friend's former lover. Nash had not known that they were already seeing each other, and when Max told him, Nash felt as if he had lost Saylor all over again. He and Max were tied to each other for the rest of their lives if they wanted to continue to co-own their business. If Max ended up with Saylor, then Nash would have to stand by and watch her move on with her life with another man. Max would live the life meant for Nash. By Saylor's side. In her arms. And in her bed.

"I can make her happy," Nash remembered Max telling him, as they sat in a fishing boat, far from the pier, engine killed and anchor down. "She needs to move on. She's held on to you with too tight of a grip. The only way she will ever be able to let go is if she loves again. I can be that man for her."

Nash could have hauled off and punched the life out of his best friend, and then thrown him overboard. Anger surfaced in his chest. Jealously raged. He didn't want his best friend's hands on the woman he loved. He would die first, or kill first, whatever it took not to have to witness it — and feel that kind of excruciating pain.

"You don't know what you are asking of me," Nash finally spoke in answer.

"You have a wife, and a baby girl. You have your life already mapped out in front of you," Max reminded him.

Nash sighed. But it wasn't what he wanted. That's not how it was supposed to be. He couldn't just turn off his feelings for Saylor. He cared about his wife, he adored his child. Even still, he had never felt the kind of love in his life, ever, as he had for Saylor.

"I know that," Nash replied. "Of all the women in the fucking world, man... why? Why mine?"

"Yours? She's not yours anymore." Max was harsh, but he didn't think twice because he believed Nash was being selfish. He couldn't possess a woman who was no longer his own. Max wanted to have a life with Saylor, and he knew he could — if he had Nash's blessing.

"You know what I mean. I'll always love her," Nash stated, as a matter of fact, and a sure as hell reality.

"But you can't have her. You gave her up. Now let her go."

Nash nodded. He didn't care if Max could see the tears welling up in his eyes. "Do you think you can love her like she deserves, and give her what she needs? Heal her, if you can. I hurt her so damn bad I can't stand it. Take the hurt away. Put that light, that fire, back in her eyes."

Back then, Max believed he could.

✱

If Things Were Different

Saylor was outside again on her front porch, seated on her favorite pale yellow rocking chair with a laptop resting on her legs. This was the first week of summer vacation for her children. She had already dropped off Syd for day camp, and Sammy of course was out riding the waves. She could see him, in the distance out in the ocean, but that wasn't why she planted herself there. At least that's what she told her son. There was, however, always an underlying fear whenever she let him surf alone. She trusted his skills, but never the hidden dangers of the water. Max reminded her time and again that their son was a natural. *Don't hold him back. My parents never did so with me. He'll be fine.*

Surprisingly, Saylor was able to focus on work out there. As long as she had her laptop with her, she could work absolutely anywhere. Most of the time that was from her home. Saylor was an experienced and successful grant writer. She was well-known and sought out in parts of North Carolina. She researched and wrote proposals for nonprofits and other organizations to receive funding from various government agencies. She had been in high demand with schools and libraries in the past few years of her career. Saylor had a knack for writing proposals to defend the reasons for funding, and the applicant's intentions. It wasn't exciting work, or hardly creative writing, but Sailor thrived at soaking up information, getting her point across, and being the reason behind others receiving free money. There was a satisfaction in her job that Saylor hoped she would never lose. The fact that she was a do-gooder had inspired her to carry on as a grant writer. If she was turned down, she only tried again, and tried harder. Rejection had changed her a long time ago. She loathed the feeling of losing. She wanted to be successful and well-liked for her mind and her skills. And she certainly was.

Saylor was so focused on flipping from two different screens on her computer. One was the research she had been reading for scholastic grants that supported both private and public libraries for programs and initiatives to help young people. The other was her blank document she had created and began to type the words she hoped would gain another successful grant. She was so intently punching the keys on her laptop that she had not seen or heard Sammy walk up. He was dripping wet, as he propped his surfboard against the column directly in front of her.

"Oh hey," Saylor looked up, as she spoke.

"Are you out here to keep tabs on me?" Sammy asked her.

She smiled. "Do I look like a worried sick mother?"

"Actually, no. You look busy."

"I am. I work well out here quite a bit." Saylor looked back down at the words she had just typed on the screen in front of her.

"I'm headed back to the beach," Sammy told her, and she half heard him, but nodded. It's when he started to walk away, that she stopped him.

"Hey, wait. What's back at the beach? I thought you were done?"

"Done surfing, but um, a few friends are waiting for me now." Sammy looked uncomfortable, or embarrassed. This was

If Things Were Different

an awkwardness that Saylor noticed about him from time to time. She looked toward the beach, and suddenly knew why her son was eager to get back out there, and probably not wanting to be seen talking to his mother. There was a cluster of teenagers, with a few girls wearing bikinis in the mix.

"Oh, I see," Saylor teased him, and he blushed.

"Mom, stop. Don't embarrass me."

"Me? Never." She smiled, and she actually meant it. "Go. Have fun."

"Thanks." He started to step away from the porch and onto the narrow cobblestone path that led out to the sand and the beach.

"Sammy," Saylor reversed his attention back to her again, "is there anyone special in that group? A pretty girl, maybe?"

"We're just friends, but maybe," he admitted with a smile that reminded her so much of Max's. "She's wearing a blue bikini today," he added, without turning around to face his mother.

"You better go say hi," Saylor giggled, and watched her son run off.

She sat there for a moment. Her mind was not at all on the grant anymore. Sammy was only four years younger than she was when she fell in love, on that very beach, for the first time. *Real love. Feelings, and a man, that she had never been able to forget.* She hoped for both of her children to find that exhilarating feeling one day. There certainly was nothing like it. No matter how short-lived or long-lasting it was.

4

There was rarely a time when Saylor was writing that the words didn't flow. She never stared blankly at a flashing cursor on the screen. She always seemed to know what she wanted to say, and then she would move on to the next grant. Research and write. That's how the hours productively passed for her during a work day. And today was no different. Syd didn't need to be picked up from day camp until late afternoon. Sammy would probably hang out with his friends, like teenagers do, for most of the day. And Max would be home in time for dinner. Many times he went back to M&N afterward, but he always said it was important to him to have that family time every evening while they ate a meal. Saylor often smiled at the thought of how they were as a family — close-knit with a dash of old-fashioned values when it came to some things. There weren't many families left like that anymore. Life was just too busy and too hectic for everyone to have the time to be at home and share food and conversation at the end of every single day.

The activity on the beach rarely distracted her, but for some reason Saylor looked up from her screen and stared out there. She saw a young woman running in the sand, close to the edge of the shore where the water washed up but had not quite reached her running shoes. Her long dark hair was pulled back in a high ponytail. It was summer time and kids were home from college. It had been months since Saylor had seen Mia but sometimes, especially during a moment like this when she had time to stare and not speak, she flashed back in her mind nearly two decades. Mia was a flawless replica of Londyn. She had her mother's dark hair and striking features, including a body with legs up to her neck. Saylor loved Mia. It didn't matter if Mia was the reason that she lost Nash all those years ago. She was a part of him, and it was fully evident. Mia may have looked like Londyn, but she had her father's warm, infectious smile and kind heart. She was an old soul with wisdom that drew people in whenever she spoke. And right now, Saylor caught her eye, and watched Mia wave, as she took a detour through the sand and sprinted up to the cobblestone sidewalk that led to the cottage.

Saylor stood up, in her powder blue cotton romper and bare feet, as Mia made her way up the three wide steps and onto the front porch. "Saylor! It's so good to see you." Mia smiled. *That infectious, familiar smile.* And Saylor opened her arms to her. Mia towered Saylor's short frame. She was every bit as tall as Londyn's five-eight-and-a-half-inch frame.

"Oh gosh, I'm sweaty, but I do want to squeeze you," Mia spoke honestly.

"Nonsense. I'm raising a teenage boy. I'm not afraid of sweat." They giggled in unison and held each other close. Mia wore a dark pink tank top and short, black spandex that hardly covered the top of her quads. "So, are you home for the summer, honey? What's the plan? An internship yet? Or a summer job?" Saylor felt completely comfortable asking Mia those questions. As if she was family. Oddly, she felt like it to Saylor. And if anyone had asked Mia, she would wholeheartedly agree.

"I'm only home for three weeks, and then I'm going back to college to start clinicals." Mia had just completed her first year at the University of North Carolina School of Medicine, where she was studying to be a pediatric nurse.

"That a girl. You're on top of your game already! And that doesn't surprise me at all. I'm proud of you, I hope you know."

"I know," Mia smiled wide at the compliment. "Thank you."

"Wanna sit?" Saylor offered her a vacant yellow rocking chair.

Mia eyed the laptop. "You're working, and I should continue my run. I told my mother I would be back, showered and ready, in time to go out to lunch with her."

Saylor nodded her head. "I'm sure Londyn is thrilled to have you all to herself for the next few weeks, but do come back here to see Syd —and Sammy— for a few hours or spend a day with us."

"I will," Mia agreed, and she meant it. She had doted on and loved five-year-old Syd since she was a baby, and even babysat her occasionally during her high school years. Sammy also was like the little brother she never had, even though in recent years he seemed to notice her as more of a young woman. Mia sensed he crushed on her at times. She shrugged it off as cute, because she already loved Sammy in that next-of-kin kind of way. "I just hope I have time to see some friends and hang out here on the beach," Mia paused, and Saylor listened. Saylor always listened. And Mia had been drawn to that trait in her over the years. "Mom is really down."

Saylor and Mia rarely ever discussed anything private about Londyn. This was new for Saylor, and she found it odd to even imagine the upbeat, all-is-well-with-the-world Londyn ever being depressed about anything. She was entirely confident about herself — and life. "Is everything okay?" Saylor asked, because she really didn't know how else to approach that.

"Modeling hasn't been going so well for her," Mia admitted. "She lost out to another, younger model for a job she really thought she would have for the summer." Londyn had modeled since she was sixteen years old. She spoke of her work a lot, but never about the pressure of aging in the business. Saylor once brought up that topic to Londyn, but she had shrugged her off. Again, her confidence carried her through everything, or so Saylor had believed.

"Your mother is beautiful," Saylor offered in all honesty.

"Yes, but she's also almost forty years old. The market is for younger, prettier…"

"There's still a need out there to capture the beauty of women *my age*," Saylor stressed with a wink at Mia. "If anything, a woman who has taken such phenomenal care of herself, like your mom has, should be a lesson for all of us."

"What are you talking about? You're gorgeous! Look at those curves on your tanned body, and definition in your leg muscles. I could run twenty miles a day and never have the legs you have. Not to mention your great tan." Mia giggled aloud because she too, like Londyn, was more on the pale, porcelain side. And Saylor looked utterly flattered.

"I do believe a compliment like that will get you anywhere with me, young lady," Saylor giggled.

"I can see why my dad fell so hard for you." Those words, from Mia, had instantly stunned Saylor. Nothing like that had ever been spoken between them before. And it should not have been. That was private. The era of Nash and Saylor as a couple was in the past. Their love affair was history. At least it was supposed to be to everyone else. No one had any clue of how Saylor still festered those feelings for Nash. Saylor felt her cheeks flush, and she was speechless, but she knew she needed to address what Mia had just spoken to her.

"What did you just say?" Saylor asked, as a way to begin again with this awkward conversation.

"I know about you and dad… and how I came along and threw things off course, to say the least."

"You are a blessing to your parents, to all of us," Saylor said, in an attempt to sway Mia from any negativity or dark thoughts.

"Don't think that," Mia read her mind. "I'm not at all self destructing. I've known the story for a few years. I just never knew how to mention it to you before," Mia stated. And Saylor wondered why she brought it up now. She had to get going. She was supposed to have lunch with her mother. This wasn't a topic to bring up, to just spit out, and then walk (or run) away.

"So I assume your mom told you when you were old enough to understand?" That didn't make complete sense to Saylor. *Why would a mother tell her child that she was an accident or a surprise which had altered her father's other love life?*

"No, actually, dad did."

Saylor's eyes widened. "Why?"

"Mom has no idea that I know," Mia said, and Saylor wasn't entirely surprised by her revelation of Londyn being unaware of something said between Mia and Nash. The two of them were close. They shared a special father-daughter bond. But the topic they shared, however, did astonish Saylor more than she wanted to admit. "Remember Jake?" Mia asked, and Saylor had. She nodded. He was the boy that Mia had fallen for when she was sixteen years old. He was her first kiss, and her first broken heart. "When I lost myself for awhile over Jake, my dad was there for me like no one else. He told me your story, yours and his."

"I'm not sure I'm comfortable with you knowing that, or just with talking about it in general with you," Saylor admitted.

"I'm not a little girl anymore, Saylor. I understand love."

"Of course, and that's not at all what I'm implying. It's me. I just... well, it was a very difficult time in my life." Saylor wanted to be honest without baring her soul to Nash's daughter.

"I admire you for many reasons, but for what you did... for me... and for my parents to be together as a family with me... was selfless." Mia's words were wise. Saylor smiled at this young, brilliant woman.

"I think you should admire your dad most. He's the one who did the right thing." Saylor could have choked on her own words. To this day, letting go of their love had never felt like the right thing to her.

"I do," Mia replied. "He knows I do."

"Your mother was very strong throughout everything too," Saylor attempted to add a few points Londyn's way.

"I love my mom," Mia stated, "but I'm not sure I could live the way she has." Saylor looked confused, as Mia finished speaking. "In someone else's shadow. Knowing her husband loved another woman, and probably would not have ever left her if it hadn't been for a baby conceived accidently."

"Mia, you are here for a reason. You have touched all of our lives. What your dad and I had was extremely special, but we were nineteen. We were kids. Believe it or not, you may feel like an adult now, but just wait until another decade, and then another, passes. Then you'll feel even more like one."

"So you're saying that young love isn't the same, or it doesn't matter as much?" Mia put Saylor in an uneasy place again.

Saylor could not lie. It mattered. Time passage had not changed her feelings in the least. Her love for Nash was built strong and remained that way. Year after passing year. "I think there's no difference between young love and mature love. If it's real, it will sustain time. I also think that some things, some people, just are not meant to be."

Mia nodded. "I didn't mean to spring this on you. It was unfair of me to make you feel like this was some sort of confrontation. I apologize. I don't mean any disrespect to you — or Max."

Saylor waved her hand at Mia. "That's ridiculous. You can talk to me about anything. No need to be sorry." With that said, Saylor still felt jittery discussing this with Mia.

"I don't know what I expected you to say to me," Mia continued. "I know how my dad feels about it. I guess I just assumed you would share his regret."

"Regret?" Saylor asked. She wanted to shake the shoulders of her former lover's daughter and demand that she tell her everything. *Was Nash still living in the past? Their past? Did he still have feelings for her? Did he miss the two of them as much as she had all of these years? Did he still love her, too?* Instead, Saylor remained calm and collected. Or at least she pretended to be.

"He told me that sometimes there's a cosmic pull between two people. You can't ignore it, and even when you try to, you're still going to be drawn together like gravity. He said that he believes in fate having a way of circling back over the paths that we are meant to cross," Mia paused. "I think my dad is a true romantic. And I also think that you understand exactly what I'm saying." Mia started to back off of the porch.

Saylor wanted to yell after her... *You cannot just leave me hanging with those words. Do you have any idea how much I will over think them now?* Instead, Saylor forced laughter from her body, deep from the pit of her stomach, and she said, "I'd like to add to those words of opinion, or wisdom — whatever they are." Mia stepped off the front porch and turned around to look back and up at Saylor. "Life is fleeting. Change can be hurled at you in a moment's notice. If you want something, or someone, don't let anyone stand in your way. Promise me you won't."

Saylor watched Mia place her hand over her heart, and before she took off sprinting down the cobblestone sidewalk, she heard Mia call out to her, "I love you, Saylor Bach!"

"And I love you, Mia Parker." And she always had. Despite how she had come into this world, and how her existence had rocked and forever changed Saylor's life.

5

Two weeks passed, and while Saylor had dwelled on and rehashed her conversation with Mia in her mind, she still managed to push her feelings deep down into her soul, and locked them there again. It wasn't a healthy way to live, but for Saylor it had been the only way.

She was stepping off her front porch, about to leave the cottage for a few hours to run errands while her children were busy doing other things without her, when her cell phone buzzed in her handbag. Saylor reached for it after she had made it to the bottom of the porch. She saw that Max was calling her.

"Hey," she spoke in answer.

"Honey, I need a favor. Are you at home?" Max's voice was typically calm, but this time was one of those instances when he sounded stressed or anxious. Saylor assumed it was work that overwhelmed him today.

"Just leaving, but still here, yes."

If Things Were Different

"I forgot my meds this morning, and today isn't a day to do without, if you know what I mean. Could you grab one and drive it over to me? Soon?"

"I will. Hang tight." She was just ten minutes away. When they ended their call, Saylor made her way back into the cottage and into the kitchen, where she twisted off the cap of a bottle of Prozac. The man ran a successful, but demanding business. He was bound to need anxiety medication to function. That was the excuse he had used for Saylor to understand his need for anti-anxiety drugs. Truth be told, his nervous nature didn't have everything to do with his business. He had started taking Prozac a few years after they were married, when his wife called out another man's name in her restless sleep. It was obvious to him the kind of dream Saylor was having in their bed. It was hardly a nightmare. But it was precisely that for Max. What he once feared was in fact true. His wife had never gotten over loving his best friend.

Saylor drove over the speed limit and made it there in less than ten minutes. Seven to be exact. She got out of her hard top white jeep and made her way to the entrance of the building. Rarely did she ever stop by to see Max at work. It just wasn't appropriate. She never wanted to be known as the little woman, the wife of the head honcho, who was there too often for no warranted reason. She wore a white sundress and flat-heeled brown gladiator sandals on her feet. Her toenails were painted fluorescent pink, and her short bob of blonde hair was bouncy on her head as she walked.

When she hustled through the main lobby, she spotted Penny — their company's administrative assistant for the past decade. Penny greeted Saylor first, and then there was an immediate unspoken exchange between them. Saylor was in a rush to get to her husband. Penny knew why she was there. Skip the small talk, and just go. "Max is expecting you. Go on in."

Saylor walked the long corridor, turned a corner, and pushed open her husband's office door. Just as she did, he got up from the chair behind his desk. He already had a bottle of water in his hand.

"Here," she handed him the lone pill from the side pocket of her handbag. He took it from her, instantly popped it into his mouth, and swallowed it down with one gulp of water.

"Can't thank you enough for rushing over," Max sighed, and Saylor noticed the sweat beads on his forehead.

"Glad I could. Listen, take a few deep breaths. Would you like to step out on the grounds for a short walk or something with me?" Saylor suggested. She didn't understand anxiety, but yet she was sympathetic of his issues with it.

Max shook his head in rejection. "No, I can't. I have too much to do today. I'll see you at dinner?"

She nodded. That was her cue to leave. They weren't the kind of couple who stole kisses behind closed doors in a place where passion could feel more exciting. She chided herself for even imagining that right now. Max needed to think straight, not fall farther off course. So she left him in his office with a mere wave of her hand as he walked back behind his desk.

If Things Were Different

Saylor closed the door behind her and took a few steps to turn the nearest corner when she ran smack into the tight, fit, broad chest which belonged to Nash. Her open palms pushed off of him and he instantly caught her by the shoulders. Physical contact rarely ever happened between them. Even quick hugs — exchanged amongst the four of them when they were tipsy or sober as they've celebrated success of their business, and friendship, over the years — were not a good idea. Physical touch stirred up too much between her and Nash.

Saylor looked up, her face flushed.

"Oh gosh, Saylor! I'm sorry. I wasn't watching where the hell I was walking. Are you okay?" He removed his hands from her bare shoulders, but the tingly sensation that he caused remained.

Saylor waved her hand in front of him. "No, my fault. I'm fine." She wasn't injured, just incredibly flustered at the moment.

"Well good," he said, as his face broke out into a wide smile. *Jesus. That smile.*

"I just had to see Max for a minute."

"Everything's okay, I hope?" Nash knew she rarely stopped by. He wished she would more often though. Seeing her brightened his day.

Saylor nodded. "All good. He just forgot something at home, and didn't have time to go back." That something was private between a husband and wife. Saylor doubted that Nash knew of Max's anxiety issues. Or maybe he had. But, either way, it wasn't her place to tell him.

"I see," Nash stated, and Saylor recognized how he wanted to say more. Perhaps to keep her there, talking and just existing toe-to-toe for a little while longer. "Mia mentioned having some plans with you and the kids before she takes off again."

"Yes, she's spending an evening with us at the end of the week. We're excited to see her again. I saw her a day or so after she got back, and we caught up for a little while on my front porch. She was running on the beach and spotted me."

Nash stood there listening. He wore pride on his face. And he wore it well. It warmed Saylor's heart through the years to see him react to his daughter. He was a wonderful, caring, and supportive father. Saylor often wondered why he and Londyn never had any more children together. It was a subject she would never address with either of them though. Because that was private between a husband and wife.

"She adores you," Nash added.

"Ahh, the feeling is completely mutual. You raised a good girl, Nash. She's going to do great things, like change the world." Saylor smiled, and Nash's eyes were bright. Gleaming with pride for sure.

"She definitely changed mine. Ours, if you really want to get matter-of-fact." Suddenly they both lost their smiles.

"Blessings aren't always evident, at first..." Saylor stated, and they both knew the truth in that.

If Things Were Different

"I agree. I don't know what I would do without my girl. She's my reason." Saylor stared up at him for a moment. Nash never said he didn't know what he would do without his family, or his wife. Just Mia. Just his daughter. She forced herself to redirect her focus, her thoughts, on something else.

"That's how we feel as parents," Saylor related. "Our children become our lives. Who knew we would end up so responsible and boring?" Saylor laughed out loud, and it made Nash chuckle at the way she always threw her head back and belted out laughter whenever she said something funny.

"Responsible and boring sounds like we are getting old," he teased her.

"Not us," Saylor laughed again. Much of her nervousness had subsided now.

"Would you like to step out on the grounds for a minute or so? Take a walk with me, maybe? I need some fresh air after being cooped up in this building all morning." His suggestion was one that Saylor had just offered to Max, and he had wanted no part of it. He preferred to pop a pill to bring calm and clear headedness. Saylor and Nash were on the same page. Fresh air, a break, just stepping away for a moment or so, always did them some good.

She caught herself nodding her head in agreement. She knew she shouldn't, but there was something about being responsible and boring that suddenly didn't appeal to her.

6

Saylor ignored the voice of reason — or warning — inside of her head as she walked through the lobby with Nash, and out the door of the front entrance. She was being reckless by Nash's side, agreeing to be alone with him. People would talk. Their employees would notice and whisper behind their backs. *Would those who knew their past history, their story, mock Max?* She was upsetting herself with unnecessary worry. Most people chalked up first loves or young love as trivial, not even close to the real thing once adulthood and maturity was reached. *She had been married to Max for fifteen years for chrissakes! She was in it with him for the long haul.*

If Things Were Different

"This isn't at all like us to do this," Saylor spoke, and Nash grinned. Her direct honesty was still one of her most admirable qualities.

"I guess that's because neither one of us have ever initiated it. We do things as a group, with Max and Londyn, to avoid being alone together and sharing what we are really feeling. Am I not right?" Now Nash was being the direct and honest one.

"So why is today different?" Saylor had to ask him, and she also ignored his question that was only going to sink them both into trouble.

"I want to talk to you about something that's going on with me," Nash began, as they started to walk to the edge of the vast parking lot near a grassy area. There were random benches, picnic tables, and one gazebo on the grounds for which the staff at M&N used during their lunch break on beautiful weather days. Saylor doubted that Max ever took advantage of those amenities out there, but she could see Nash kicking off his shoes and doing so.

For a moment, Saylor felt alarmed. "Nash, you're scaring me. It's not your health, is it?"

"I'm fine," he smiled at her, and she noted again that his light brown hair was overgrown. But it suited him. It enhanced his wild, sexy side. The immediate concern she still had for him warmed Nash's heart, and another area below his belt. "My life is changing, and I've had a lot of time this past year to reevaluate what that feels like, and what it means." Saylor listened raptly, as they continued to walk the grounds. They were now stepping in the grass and near a picnic table. Nash climbed up on it first and then sat on top of the table, with his feet planted on the bench. Leave it to him to be different. To be both boyish and manly. Saylor acted like a lady and sat down on the bench and spun her legs underneath the table. She rested her elbows on the tabletop and looked up at him. She was aware that he could see down the front of her scoop neck sundress right now. She liked the feeling of knowing that, and wondering if she still excited him in that way. *He noticed, and yes she had.*

"Nash, I want to hear what you have to say, I want to know what's weighing on your mind. But, us, out here like this? What if Max peers out of his office window and sees us?"

Nash chuckled a little at her terrible sense of direction. "His office is on the south side of the building. Our location is currently the north side."

Saylor rolled her eyes at him, knowing he was making fun of her, and he chuckled aloud again. "Okay, okay. Tell me what's bothering you."

"Londyn and I have an empty nest. Our daughter is already, in a sense, on her own. Our house, those massive rooms on every floor, is just too big. The space between us is no longer filled with Mia. She was our middle ground. She was our conversation piece. She was our reason."

"I'm not sure what you're getting at," Saylor admitted. "I've heard of parents having a hard time with their children being gone and having a quiet house where it's just the two of them again, like how it all initially began."

If Things Were Different

"Right," Nash spoke up, "for most people, but that's not how it began for Londyn and me. We wouldn't even be together, married, sharing a life, if it had not been for Mia's existence."

"Should you be telling me this, Nash? Are you going to leave Londyn because raising your daughter together feels like it's come to an end?" Saylor was suddenly afraid of what his answer was going to be. "Doesn't she mean more to you than that?"

Nash sighed. "I've had an entire year of these thoughts going back and forth in my mind. I have to tell someone. I think you know why I'm telling you. I love Londyn. I have grown to genuinely love her and care about her. I'm just not in love with her, and I'm not ever going to be. I've felt what that feels like. It can't be forced or faked. I've spent two decades of my life doing what I am supposed to do, being where I never believed I was meant to be, but I've stayed anyway. Now, our glue, Mia, is no longer holding us together. She's practically an adult. She gets me. I don't think she will be surprised or devastated if I leave her mother. Mia knows I would never abandon her."

Saylor shook her head repeatedly and stood up and then got out from having her legs confined underneath the picnic table. She paced the grassy area in front of it, and finally looked back at Nash, still seated on top. He didn't seem the least bit rattled by what he told her.

"You have to respect the fact that I am married," There. She said it. She just went ahead and spoke what was on her mind, and obviously Nash's as well. "My situation is not at all comparable to yours. What's happening between you and

Londyn has nothing to do with Max and me. My husband doesn't deserve this. The way you are talking, what you are implying—"

Nash held up his hand. "I'm not asking anything of you. Max is my best friend and business partner. There's a lot at stake here. I just wanted to tell someone, you, that I'm not happy with the direction of my life. I did my part as a father, and I will continue to, but I can't be her husband anymore. You have to know that I love your family, the family you created with Max. I don't want to hurt anyone." Saylor nodded, and Nash continued. "But the fact that you assumed as much about me, about what I could be asking of you, makes me wonder how much you've really moved on in your life also."

"That's not fair," Saylor spoke, trying not to snap at him. But this angered her, he stirred a fury in her, because she knew he was right. "Max has been nothing but good to me, and he's a wonderful, supportive, and loving father to both of our children."

"I know all of that. I didn't ask about Max," Nash spoke to her in a serious business-like tone. "I asked about you. There's a significant difference between having a man love you and nurture you and your children — and having a man reach your soul." Nash had just implied that they were soul mates. And Saylor didn't call him out, or disagree.

"I never see myself leaving him, if that's what you are asking," she carefully and somewhat vaguely answered his question without admitting her true feelings for him that had never diminished.

If Things Were Different

"I understand," Nash stated. "I love him, too, you know? Enough to give him my blessing all those years ago, when really all I wanted to do was kill him for taking you away, and seizing the life I was supposed to have with you."

"I'm not some kind of prized possession that one of you gave up and the other won," Saylor was upset at the thought of him and Max fighting over her. "I chose Max to be my husband."

"I told him to heal you. I told him to put that light, that spark, back in your eyes again after I had taken it away." Saylor swallowed hard the lump rising in her throat, and she felt the tears fill up in her eyes. "I never saw that come back for you. I saw happiness, fulfillment, and contentment that he and your children have brought to your life. But I never saw that fire return in you. Not once."

A few tears rolled down her cheeks and dripped off her face. Nash stared at her. The way her blonde hair caressed the underside of her jawbone. He wanted to reach out and tuck her hair back behind her ears and press his lips to hers. "That's because it, that fire in my soul, burned out the moment you broke me."

Nash jumped off of the tabletop. "I swear to God I've lived with that regret every day since." He stepped closer to her. And she didn't back away.

"I know you have," she told him. "I haven't forgotten you, or moved past thinking about what we shared." She thought of him when her husband touched her. She dreamed about him all night long after she was made love to by another man. "I've never gotten over you, Nash, and I never will. But that's where those feelings have to stay."

Nash wanted so badly to reach for her, to touch her, to pull her close and kiss her. But he kept still, and stayed silent. And then he watched her walk away from him. What Saylor had said to him was enough. For now. He waited two decades to hear those words from her, to know she felt the exact same way as he still did.

7

Saylor was rattled and still feeling on edge that evening after dinner. Max had gone out surfing with Sammy. She and Syd were inside the cottage playing the Chutes and Ladders board game on the glass-topped wagon wheel table in front of the sofa. Sammy later returned, dripping wet, and looking to change out of his swim trunks and into dry clothes for a late-night hangout on the beach. Once he left, and Saylor had tucked Syd into bed, she walked out onto the front porch and found Max sitting on one of the rockers. His dark hair was still damp, a towel covered his shoulders, and his bare chest and red swim trunks were visible. She sat down in the rocking chair adjacent to him.

"Syd fell asleep already. Summer time is wearing her out," Saylor giggled, as she curled her legs underneath her bottom.

Max smiled. "She likes to stay busy, that's for sure."

"And what are you so busy thinking about out here, all alone?" Saylor asked him.

"Life," he answered, and already he had Saylor's undivided attention. "We get so wrapped up in the day-to-day things we have to do to survive, that we forget to stop and enjoy everything else." Saylor understood, but she didn't completely agree with him, because she knew how to balance what she had to do, and what she wanted to do. Work hard, but take the time to have fun. She also tried very hard to instill that into her children. She witnessed how hard Max worked, and she was grateful to him for providing in spades for his family, as well as giving so many others jobs within his company so that they could make better than decent livings.

"Sounds like you need a little break from life. Do you want to take a vacation somewhere with the kids, or maybe just us?" Saylor suddenly felt excited. It had been several years, before Syd was born, since they had traveled anywhere.

"I can't get away that long," Max spoke as if he believed that, and Saylor thought of the many times throughout the years when Nash left the company solely for Max to handle while he, Londyn and Mia took various trips. Mia was only nineteen years old and she had been on an airplane at least a dozen times in her life.

If Things Were Different

"Then what?" Saylor asked him, feeling a little miffed. "What do you need to get out of this slump?"

Max shrugged, and his towel fell loose from one shoulder. "Nash told me he wants to leave Londyn." That was it. That was what weighed heavily on his mind tonight.

Saylor nodded. "I know. He told me, too. I bumped into him in the hallway today when I left your office." Literally, she had *bumped into* him. "He feels like his life has come to a crossroad. I think a lot of people have trouble dealing with the empty nest stage of life. Couples need to have a strong marriage to survive that change, I guess."

"I think Londyn is going to be devastated," Max spoke in her defense.

"Probably," Saylor replied, "but we don't know that for sure. Maybe she would welcome that change, too?"

"What?" Max nearly snapped at her. "Londyn is crazy over him, and he's being an arrogant SOB. Does he really think he can start his life over at almost forty years old and have any woman he wants?" Saylor didn't know how to answer that, because she believed Nash was a good looking, youthful man still. And he was charming. *But, as far as having any woman he wanted... well, Nash wanted her. And no, he couldn't have her anymore. Could he?*

"I don't think that's really our business, it's certainly not our place to judge what will or will not make someone else happy," Saylor said vaguely, as if they weren't speaking about a significant person in their lives.

"I understand that," Max told her, "it's his life. But, to hear him speak right now, it's like he thinks he's paid his dues. He played the good, faithful husband and doting daddy throughout the years and now that his daughter is no longer a child, he's free to go?"

Saylor nodded. "I know. But we can't change how he feels, and to be honest, I really have not gotten close enough to Londyn to know how she might feel." *Or to care*, Saylor thought.

"But you know how Nash feels?" he asked her point blank.

"What?" Saylor replied.

"Would you leave me for him?" Max spoke those words almost as nonchalantly as if he was asking her if she wanted take-out for dinner.

"Why ask me something like that, Max? We have quite the life together with our children. I'm happy just where I am. Don't insult me just because Nash and I used to be involved, and now that he may be free you're questioning my loyalty to you and our family?" Saylor should have felt somewhat guilty, considering that she had confessed her festering feelings to Nash just hours earlier today, but she didn't. Because she had told Nash the very same thing she was telling her husband now. She was not going to run to him and be with him. She would not sacrifice her marriage and her family for him.

"You're right, I'm sorry," Max spoke sincerely. "I guess some of those insecurities surfaced again today. I mean, I know you loved him, and if Mia had not come along—"

If Things Were Different

"That was too long ago to matter anymore," Saylor heard herself say to her husband. If only she believed those words. But that notion never sunk in — to her head, or her heart. Ever. Saylor moved her tanned legs in cut-off denim shorts from underneath her. She planted her bare feet on the porch floorboards. She stood up and walked over to Max, and then held out her hand to him. He didn't hesitate to hold it, and intertwine his fingers with hers. "Come inside. Let's go to bed. I want to remind you how much you mean to me."

Max stood up, and left behind his wet towel on the yellow rocking chair. Reconnecting with his wife was exactly what he needed to get past the hold that he believed Nash Parker would always have on their life. And Saylor.

*

All eyes were on Mia as she sat at the Bach's dinner table at the cottage. They were eating grilled shrimp, fillets, brown rice, and spinach salad. When she spoke, she held all of their interest. She told them how her love of babies all of her life — and persistent guidance from her father — had put her on the path of wanting to become a pediatric nurse. She was clearly intelligent, and Nash had always told her *to choose some type of career in the medical field. You will not only make money, you'll feed your need to make a difference.*

"So I can partially blame my dad when I end up working my life away because nurses never get a weekend or a holiday off!" Mia over exaggerated, maybe a little.

"That just may be a reality for you until you pay your dues, and work your way up the seniority ladder," Max told her. He certainly knew about making sacrifices for his career throughout the number of years that he was overworked when he and Nash built their business from the ground up.

Saylor watched as Max interacted with Mia. Saylor could tell that Max was taken by her, and genuinely cared about her. Mia definitely had her mother's striking beauty, but she was all Nash in the eloquent way that she spoke. She was expressive and captivating. Oddly, Saylor felt as proud of Mia as she had her own children. Mia wasn't a child anymore. She was a young lady, on her way to doing great things with her life. The world was at her feet. She could be anything she wanted. And the fact that she realized that already at nineteen years old was remarkable. Mia caught Saylor smiling and admiring her, and for a brief second the two of them shared a moment. Saylor winked at her, and Mia held her gaze and smiled wide.

After dinner, Max went back to the office. Before he did, he enveloped Mia in his fatherly arms and wished her well with clinicals all summer long. Saylor allowed Syd to play one board game with Mia and Sammy. Sammy joined in, but hardly concentrated on the game as he talked nonstop about surfing. He was headed out to the water again before dark. Mia seemed intrigued by his continuous surf talk. She wasn't an avid surfer anymore, but she once was and she was experienced after living near the water all of her life.

If Things Were Different

"Come out with me sometime, if you're back for a visit this summer over a weekend or maybe the 4th of July holiday?" Saylor heard Sammy's suggestion as she walked from the kitchen into the living area. Her children and Mia were seated on the floor in front of the sofa.

"That sounds amazing. Too enticing to wait," Mia responded, and then she tugged at the strap of her swimsuit from underneath her tank top. "I do have my bathing suit on tonight. I wanted to be prepared for a swim...but surfing sounds much more exciting."

"Oh, I don't know," Saylor chimed in. "Just go for a swim with her Sammy. It's too late in the day to surf anyway."

"Seriously mom? This is the time of day I enjoy it most." Sammy was instantly annoyed, and adamant.

"I'm not talking about you," Saylor told her son, and he obviously never picked up on her serious, parental tone.

"I need to learn to live it up more when I can, when moments like this are staring me in the face," Mia said to Saylor. "College has been pretty intense and mostly serious for me. I'm not there to party like so many of my friends. My own roommate is too hung-over three days out of five to get to her morning classes on time."

Saylor failed at suppressing a giggle. She remembered those carefree, or careless, days all too well. She didn't want to mother Mia. She had Londyn for that. Saylor wanted Mia to let loose and enjoy life sometimes. She was too young to be saddled with being a responsible adult already. Of course, she should study hard and set goals. But life, especially at nineteen, shouldn't be all work and no play.

"You might want to check with your parents first," Saylor said, pretty much granting both her and Sammy permission to surf after all.

"Oh," Mia waved her hand in front of her face, "it's fine."

When Sammy practically skipped out of the room to go change into his swim trunks, Saylor watched Syd crawl up onto Mia's lap. Mia held her close and kissed her on top of her full head of blonde curls. "I want you to have lots of fun this summer and I will come back to see you again soon, okay?"

Syd nodded her head. "And we can play more board games?"

"Absolutely!" They hugged again, and Saylor felt teary when Mia said, "I love you, kiddo." It was uncanny how life worked out for all of them. In the beginning of their story, a baby had permanently torn Saylor away from Nash, but somehow they all had remained connected and became family over the years. Max and Nash were close friends and successful business partners. Their children, all three of them, loved each other like siblings. Saylor realized that Londyn tried really hard to be a part of their closeness, that bond. And while watching Mia now, Saylor felt a little pang of guilt in her chest. Maybe it was time for her to be more willing to accept Londyn for who she was? Londyn, after all, gave them this beautiful girl who they each loved so very much. Saylor instantly made up her mind. She was going to put forth her best effort to convince Nash to give Londyn and their marriage another try. She might even call up Londyn and invite her to lunch, considering her summer was going to be lonelier than she had planned — with

If Things Were Different

no modeling gig, and Mia absent from home.

On the front porch, Saylor shared an embrace with Mia that was affectionate and meaningful. *Goodbye for now.* Mia expressed her gratitude for a wonderful dinner, and Saylor reminded her that she was welcome *anytime*.

"Be safe out there," she called to them as they stepped off the porch and each grabbed ahold of and carried a surfboard. Saylor sat down on the yellow rocking chair with a tired Syd on her lap. She wanted to be out there on that porch for awhile. Both Sammy and Mia knew to come back before sunset. Saylor told herself they would be fine. She could hear Max's voice in her head, reminding her, *Don't hold him back. He's a natural born surfer. He'll be fine.* Well it wasn't just Sammy out there on the water. Mia was along.

*

Saylor walked along the edge of the shore. It was windy and the waves were coming in fast and rough, crashing at her ankles, and splashing up to her bare legs. She still wanted to, and continued to, find such serenity near the ocean.

Her thoughts were pained and troublesome, but that was how life had been the last several, excruciating days. Saylor rehashed everything in her mind. It was too much to rethink. But it's what she did. It's how she coped. And ultimately survived. She couldn't change anything, but she still drummed up the ways that perhaps could have altered a tragic outcome out there on the water, trapped under those tides. With her entire being, Saylor desperately wished things were different. She ached unbelievably so from this loss.

Blame was a harsh thing. Pointing fingers. Lashing out. Perhaps it was a coping mechanism for some in the throes of agony. Saylor could still see Max's face that night. And Londyn's. And Nash's.

She was the *adult in charge!* Max had screamed at her.

Mia had not surfed in a very long time. She was out of her league out there! Londyn cried.

Nash had not uttered a word, or any blame. He only stared blankly in the distance out there as the sun began to set. It was almost eerie what Saylor had been thinking when she watched him, so lost and forlorn. There was a familiar agonizing stare on his face just like the time when he was struck blindly with the news that he had a baby about to make her entrance into his world. He was rocked to his very core then. Just the same as he was the night he was told his daughter had left this world.

Those moments between frantically running off of the front porch — hurdling two of the three steps — and making her way to the beach, to the edge of the shore were all too clear in her mind. Sammy's desperate screams for help would always haunt her. He begged her to help him save Mia. But Saylor couldn't come through for her son, nor for the young woman she loved as her own child.

Sammy had pulled her in, on his surfboard. The one Mia had used, an old one of Sammy's, was lost in the water. She had wiped out when charging a wave. Her board came away, and

If Things Were Different

she had no leash. Sammy forced his way to her, but she had already been held under for two waves. He fought to reach her. He fought to get to the shore. It had been too long for Mia. Too much water had gotten into her lungs. She was drowning. Too much time had passed before Sammy finally had her body level in the sand and attempted to revive her. Saylor had shoved him back and out of the way. What he was doing was not working. She had to try. To do it better. To make something happen. Those seconds couldn't be wasted. Saylor was still pumping Mia's chest when the paramedics arrived. She reluctantly backed off. She held a distraught Sammy in her arms, with their bottoms sunken in the sand, as they watched nothing change. Nothing happened to revive, to bring back Mia. She was gone.

Max arrived first. He was in closest proximity at the time, when he was alone at the office. Nash had been at the condo with Londyn.

Max lashed out at Sammy. *You should have known better! She was incapable of handling herself out there! And there's absolutely no way you could have taken care of yourself and her on that water!*

But ultimately Max blamed Saylor. *You have got to be kidding me! You allowed this? You were the fucking parent out here!*

As awful and as hurtful as Max's words were, Londyn's were far worse. She fell to her knees in front of her daughter's drenched, lifeless body on the beach. She sobbed over her as she clung to her. She begged and pleaded with her, and bargained with God and the universe to undo this awful fate. And then she somehow mustered the strength to get to her feet, and face Saylor. Nash was there and not able to comfort his wife, as he choked on his own sobs, holding his daughter in his arms for the final time.

"You did this to my daughter because of me, didn't you?" Londyn spoke in a strangely calm tone. Saylor only stared back at her. She was a mother in wretched pain. She had a right to say whatever she wanted to say. Saylor's heart broke for her, but Londyn would never know that. "You've always hated me. My baby and I ruined your plans with Nash. We lived *your* life. How heartless can you be? It may have taken you two decades, but you did this to spite me, to hurt me in the worst way, and to take everything from me!" By now, Nash had been on his feet. He grabbed his wife from behind, yanking her back by both of her upper arms.

"That's enough!" he screamed through the tears that clouded his eyes and dampened his entire face.

Londyn managed to wriggle out of his grip and she ran off, down the beach as her daughter's body was being placed into a body bag and zipped shut as if Mia was never a living, breathing, incredible human being always so full of life. Her body was waste now. The mere thought of it was the most repulsive feeling for Saylor.

In the midst of Londyn's cruel words to Saylor, Sammy had taken off running up the beach. Max had immediately gone after him. Nash and Saylor were left there. He had yet to speak to her. She was fighting her sobs as she turned to face him. He was a broken man. It took all she had left in her not to run to him and hold him and attempt to comfort him. Instead she stood still, waiting, as the sky darkened around them. The moment the sky went black mirrored how the light of Nash's life had gone out that night.

If Things Were Different

Nash looked at her. And she back at him. Saylor was so frightened of what lied ahead, and how Nash and Londyn were ever going to survive this god-awful loss. She wondered if Max would eventually stop being so angry with her. And she was sick with worry how this tragedy was going to affect Sammy. *He was just a boy still.*

And then Nash finally spoke the only words he had said to Saylor in the aftermath of his daughter's untimely death. "This was not your fault."

8

Saylor knocked twice on Sammy's closed bedroom door before she turned the doorknob. It was locked. She knocked harder. "Sammy, open up, or I'll get the key." She heard the bed frame squeak as he got up, and a second later he turned the lock from the other side of the door. Saylor opened it and stepped inside. His room was a disaster, more than usual, as there were clothes strewn all over the floor, and empty soda cans and trash scattered across the dresser top. The blinds were completely closed to prevent sunlight inside. The mother in her wanted to raise her voice and demand that he *clean up his room! Who lived like that?* A boy who saw a girl die, that's who. And not just any girl. Mia was like a sister to him. Saylor inhaled a deep breath as Sammy sat on his bed with earbuds connected to his cell phone. He wouldn't look at her, as Saylor walked over to him and sat down on the edge of the bed near him.

If Things Were Different

"Take the earbuds out," she told him, and for a second she wondered if Sammy could hear her, or if she had just been ignored. And then she watched him release the buds from his ears simultaneously. "You've gone on like this for days," she began. "I know you are hurting, but this stops today."

Sammy only gave her fleeting eye contact before he finally spoke. "I can't just shut off the pain."

"No, none of us can," Saylor agreed with him. "We can learn to live again though. It's what Mia would want."

"What she wanted was to live. She had plans, mom. Big dreams. She was going to be a baby nurse. She told us how excited she was, remember, it's all she talked about during dinner. Why did I have to bring up surfing? I never should have invited her to go out there! You didn't think it was a good idea at first either! Why did she have to die, mom?" Sammy voice broke, and Saylor reached for his arm. She rubbed her open palm up and down his slender arm.

"I don't have the answers to any of what you are asking, but I've thought of all of it over and over since that night. Why? I'm so angry and completely devastated and I'm at a loss about what to do for Nash and Londyn, and for you and Dad, and Syd." Saylor didn't say that Max hadn't come home to have dinner with them as a family since the night they ate their last meal with Mia. She also didn't add that Syd hadn't been able to sleep through the night in her own bed since either. But most of all, she was worried about her boy. Each day he had become a little more withdrawn.

"Is dad still mad at you?"

Saylor only nodded her head.

"He shouldn't blame you. It's not your fault." Saylor thought of Nash telling her the very same thing on the beach that night.

"Thank you, honey," Saylor attempted to smile at him, but instead she only tightened her lips to fight back a cry.

"I'm never going out there again…" Sammy spoke adamantly. At first, Saylor thought he meant outside of his bedroom. She imagined how dreadful that would be. A young boy growing into a man inside of that dark, depressing teenaged bedroom. She pushed the ridiculousness of that thought out of her mind, and pressed him for more.

"The beach? The sand? The ocean water?"

"All of the above. You can sell my surfboard, because I'll never touch it again."

"Sammy," Saylor spoke calmly, "You were raised on this beach. This is not just your home, but your life. It's who you are. The sand between your toes. The wind, the waves. You are not whole unless your bare feet are planted on top of a surfboard in that water. As your mother, I have worried sick about you out there pretty much from the moment you could stand for the first time. But I've watched you. You, like your dad has always said, are a natural. If you deprive yourself of what you love most in this world, besides me," she winked, but her boy never smiled back at her, "a part of you will die inside. You are fifteen years old. I hope to live a very long time to see you grow into a man and have a wonderful life of your own. But if you lose

If Things Were Different

yourself because of this tragedy, if you lose your mindset because you lost Mia, I will refuse to watch your destruction."

"What are you saying? You'll leave us?" What Saylor said had gotten to him. She wasn't entirely sure why she had phrased it that way, but maybe there was a part of her that wanted to run from this pain just as much as Sammy wanted to hide from it.

"I can only take so much. I think I would. I would pack up Syd and just get away from here. What would I have to lose? Your dad is so pissed off at me that he only comes home to sleep. You're locked in here in the dark all day and night. If anything, Syd deserves more. She's so confused, she's just too little to understand what happened. I have to turn this family around, Sammy, and I need you to help me do it. This is awful to say, but we are all still here. You came out of that water safely. If Nash and Londyn had the chance to be a family with Mia again, I believe they would do anything to make that happen. I'm not giving up on what I have. I'm not leaving, Sammy. I'm just trying my hardest to reach you."

Sammy started to cry. Her overgrown boy of fifteen had fallen apart at the seams from a tragedy that would stay with him for the rest of his life. Saylor held him tight and close, as she too lost her composure.

✱

Saylor was torn. She wanted to reach out to Nash — and Londyn. Going to their condo would be awkward and uncomfortable. And besides, Londyn would probably slam the door in her face. The last time she had seen both of them was at Mia's funeral, when the pain and heartbreak from that day was entirely too much to bear.

When she asked Max, late the night before when he finally came home from work, if Nash had returned to work yet, he answered no. And that was the extent of their conversation. Period.

She had his number logged into her cell phone. It was there. She rarely ever used it to contact him. But right now she felt helpless. She wanted both Nash and Londyn to know that she cared. Life, after one person's tragedy, went on for everyone else. But Saylor and her family were suffering their loss with them. They would miss Mia for the rest of their lives, too. She was a part of their family. She lost her life that night just outside of their front door, down the beach and in the ocean water, in the vicinity they called their home.

Saylor sent a single, simple text to Nash.

I know you're going through pure hell. I can't bear this.

That was all. She contemplated telling him *to reach out if he needed her,* but she would have felt sneaky, and probably guilty, if she had. She just wanted to be a friend to Nash, now more than ever. It didn't help at all that Max was barely communicating with her. Saylor needed to talk about her overwhelming emotions with someone other than her children — because with them she forced herself to be strong.

If Things Were Different

Less than sixty seconds later, Saylor's phone buzzed.

Everyone keeps saying they're here if I need anything. I don't. Not from them. The fact that you miss my girl as much as I do makes me feel not as alone in this madness. Meet me. I need to talk about this before I go completely crazy.

Ironically, they were always in sync. Saylor inhaled a deep breath, and then she reread his message. Nash needed to talk about his pain, and so did she. This was dangerous territory that she was stepping into. The boundaries were going to be blurred by grief. She knew that. She told herself that. And yet, she replied to him instantly.

Where are you right now?

9

Nash's text asked her to meet him at The Waterfront Bar. Saylor was taken aback for a moment as she read those words. The Waterfront Bar was their place. Their old stomping ground. They were both underage back then, but Nash's older brother had connections there and always succeeded at sneaking them into that rustic watering hole. That bar sat on the waterfront in downtown Morehead City. Saylor remembered all too well dancing to the live music, and watching the bustling waterfront life right there on the harbor. It's a wonder now, looking back, that she and Nash never had gotten caught. Too many beers. Too much fun. And memories with him that wouldn't escape her.

If Things Were Different

It was only one o'clock in the afternoon in the middle of the work week. Saylor wondered if that was how Nash had been spending his time. Coping any way possible. Losing himself in alcohol to avoid having to feel the full extent of his sorrow.

Syd was at day camp again, and Saylor told Sammy, who was lying on the sofa watching Netflix, that she had errands to run. He was beginning to lose his summer tan already. It had faded along with his spirit. Saylor had yet to be successful at getting him to go outside, even at the very least just to feel the sun on his face. She checked her hair and makeup in the mirror. She was wearing a coral sundress with pewter flip flops on her feet. She looked ready to go out in public. *To a bar in the middle of the day?* Saylor needed to check more than her appearance. She needed a sanity check. A serious evaluation of good sense. She pushed that thought from her mind. Nash needed her.

Walking into that place, that rustic building on water, was like going back in time. Only she didn't have to stand up tall, push out her chest, or do anything else to act older so she wouldn't be spotted in the crowd and carded and thrown out. She was legal. She could be there. A dwindling lunch crowd was inside. Saylor didn't glance at every table. She had noticed Nash's vehicle parked outside, and she already assumed he was on the dock. And that he was.

She stepped outside onto the wooden dock, where some of those planks were in need of retreatment. If she looked down and focused, she could see the water flowing between the narrow gaps.

Nash was seated at a tall table for two, closest to the end of the dock near the water, and his back was to her. She stopped at his chair, and he turned to her. He may have, at first, thought she was going to be a waitress, there to refill his beer. Then again, he was waiting for her to meet him there. All she said, when her eyes met his teary ones, was "Oh Nash..."

It was unclear who initiated their embrace, who opened their arms first. All Saylor knew was that she fell into him and held on for dear life. They had not been that close for more than a matter of quick seconds in years. Their hugs or sociable pats were always very cordial and in front of their spouses. Even at the funeral, Saylor kept her distance most of the time. Londyn intentionally ignored her, and at one point Saylor had spoken briefly to and cried terribly hard with Nash. She had her family beside her at the time, and everyone had been engulfed in sadness and tears. It was more like the Bachs as a united front offering their sympathy then. Today, it was Saylor giving him all the empathy and compassion she had to offer. It was also unclear who pulled out of their embrace first, but they both eventually parted and wiped their faces dry, as Saylor sat down on the tall chair across from him.

"Thank you for being here," he spoke, clearing his throat, which had sounded raw from excessive crying. "Can I get you a drink?"

Saylor looked on the tabletop between them. He was drinking a bottled beer. "I'll have a beer, too."

Nash turned around to catch the waitress's attention at a table behind them. "Two more," he said, holding up his fingers, and his request was heard. His beer wasn't quite gone yet, but he hoped Saylor would stay long enough for him to drink another one.

"It would be ridiculous of me to ask how you are doing," Saylor began, as she looked at him. Really looked at him, this time. His light brown hair was as overgrown as always, but it was clean and styled. His white t-shirt and cargo khaki shorts both looked presentable. His face was unshaven, scruffy, and his eyes were red. That was the only giveaway for Saylor. The sadness she saw was heartbreaking.

"Awful. Sick to my stomach. All cried out. Losing her is going to do me in. I'm already done. Done with life. She was my reason. My girl is gone." It actually felt good for him to say all of that. All of what he had been thinking and feeling for several days. There was no one else to tell. From Nash's perspective, when he did go home to their condo, Londyn was worse off than him.

"I hear you, I do," Saylor began. "I believe I know you well enough to completely understand your need to want to give up. That girl, from the moment we all laid eyes on her, knew how to make us fall hard. She loved you most, you know…" Nash choked back his tears as Saylor continued speaking. He needed to hear her voice, her wise words. She always had known just what to say, exactly what he needed. "She told us, at dinner…" Saylor paused, and willed herself to keep it together. Talking about Mia was healing. It would also keep that wonderful girl's memory alive. And Saylor wanted to begin to mend his brokenness. "She said that there were two things that had put her on the path of wanting to become a pediatric nurse — her love of babies all of her life and the persistent guidance from her father. She said you always believed she was intelligent and told her to choose some type of career in the medical field, because she would not only make money, but feed her need to make a difference. She knew how proud her daddy was of her."

There were tears streaming down Nash's face. Saylor could hardly finish her words to him. "I will always be proud of her," Nash found his voice between sobs. "Just think of what she could have been, and all that she could have accomplished."

"I have been," Saylor wiped the tears pooling underneath her own eyes. The tips of her fingers now had black mascara on them. "It's so brutally unfair. I'll never get over this feeling of being robbed. We were all robbed of her. Mia was robbed of her life. My children were robbed of their sister."

Nash smiled at her. "You've never said that before. You've never implied that our kids were like siblings."

"I didn't have to. We all already knew they were." Saylor stopped to take her first drink of the bottled beer their waitress had quietly placed in front of her and then hurriedly backed away when she witnessed the two of them sharing an intensely emotional private conversation.

"How's Sammy holding up?" Nash asked her, sincerely. And it was like a dam had broken for her, inside of her heart, when he spoke out of genuine concern for her son. Saylor covered her mouth with her hand and attempted to stifle a cry, as tears dripped off her face.

"He's all but given up, too. He's heartbroken, traumatized. I don't know how else to describe it. He won't leave the cottage. He has sworn off the beach and the water. He said he'll never surf again. He has such regret for being the one out on the water with her."

Nash nodded his head. "I don't blame him for what happened. And I already told you, it wasn't your fault. Not in my eyes." Saylor knew he was indirectly referring to both Londyn and Max.

At that moment, Saylor loved this man more than she ever had in all of their intertwined years together. He had every right to force blame. To accuse. And to hate. Instead, he was the one holding out his hand and offering peace and understanding. "Thank you," was all she managed to mutter before she reached out her hand and met his on the tabletop.

After she had two beers, and he had three, it was getting close to the time she had to leave to pick up Syd from day camp. Their conversation continued to be deep and meaningful, and they had cried more tears together.

Nash saw Saylor glance at the time on her cell phone.

"You have to go, don't you? Your family awaits." He was regretful to see this afternoon end with her. And it stung a little to know that Saylor had a family waiting for her, counting on her. He lost the one person, that mattered, who depended on him.

"Syd's at day camp. I need to come up with a plan for dinner, even though Max doesn't bother to come home to eat with us anymore." As soon as she said it, Saylor wished she hadn't. Max was suffering too. Grief had affected them all in different ways.

"He's wrong to blame you. If I ever get back to work, I'll be sure to tell him that." Nash was serious. The two of them rarely held back their opinions with each other. It's why he and Max were the best of friends. They were real with each other.

"He'll come around," Saylor said, reaching into her handbag for her wallet. She had a couple of beers to pay for.

Nash held up his hand to stop her in action. "No. I got it. It's on me. It's the least I can do to thank you for showing up, day drinking with me, and being the one person I can talk to right now." That wasn't exactly a fair statement. Max had reached out to him repeatedly too, but Nash had not been very receptive with him.

"I wanted to be here," she responded. "There's no other way to say it. I want to help you through this, if you'll let me."

This was the first time in days that Nash felt a spark of life inside of him again. He was still hurting and he was far from being okay, but Saylor made him feel as if the lonely, grief-stricken road he was on was a little less hopeless. And he needed to cling to that feeling right now. ·

He stood up with her as she made the first move to transition out of there.

"You're alright to drive?" he asked her.

"I can handle two beers," she winked at him.

If Things Were Different

"That's my girl," Nash stated, and immediately caught himself, as Saylor blushed. He didn't apologize and she didn't ask him to. It had been a long damn time since she heard those words from him. Forever ago since she had been *his girl*.

She looked down for a moment at her feet, at the water rushing in between the crevices underneath that dock.

And before Saylor knew it, Nash gently lifted her chin with two of his fingers. Their eyes locked. He leaned forward. She rose up on her tip toes. Their lips met, and the rest of the world faded away.

10

Saylor sat taller behind the wheel and applied lip balm while she drove home with Syd. She thinned out her lips, she puckered them, and then she took another look. *Did they look different?* She felt self conscious, almost as if anyone would be able to take one look at her and know. It was guilt — and it had nothing to do with how her lips felt or looked.

"Mommy, are your lips chapped?" her observant child asked, from the booster seat in the back of the closed-top white jeep.

"No honey, just maybe a little sunburned," Saylor fabricated that possibility, and gave her daughter a smile in the rearview mirror.

"Do you think Sammy went outside today?" Syd innocently asked, because what was going on with her brother was on her mind.

If Things Were Different

"I don't know, but I'm sure one of these days he will. He's just not ready yet," Saylor defended her son, but she too thought it was time for him to get out of this dreadful hermit stage.

"Will daddy be home to eat dinner with us tonight?" Syd asked yet another question from the backseat. Saylor was patient with her. She was a curious five-year-old regardless, but the changes in her life lately were affecting her and she needed to be inquisitive. She wanted answers. Saylor didn't blame her. She felt primarily the same.

"I hope so," Saylor replied, honestly. "I'll call daddy when we get home to see what he's hungry for."

Syd giggled. "I'm hungry for macaroni and cheese!"

"Well you're easy enough," Saylor laughed, as she made the final turn toward their beach cottage.

*

When they arrived, Max's truck was parked there. After Syd had her moment of excitement, seeing that her *daddy was home*, Saylor pulled down the sun visor and checked her face another time in the mirror. She inhaled a deep breath through her nostrils. She fretted for a moment that her face appeared flushed from drinking alcohol, and her breath most likely reeked of it. A moment later, she followed Syd inside.

Max was standing in the kitchen. He wore red swim trunks and a black t-shirt, making his dark hair a stand-out characteristic.

"You're home," Saylor said first, after Syd ran to him and he swung her around in his arms.

"Yeah, I'm preparing to grill, if that works for you. I picked up some swordfish," Max spoke as if he had turned a corner. Like his anger toward her had finally diminished. *Of all days.* Saylor had just spent the entire afternoon with Nash. *And she kissed him!*

"Did you get some mac-n-cheese, too?" Syd squealed, her blonde curls bounced on her head as she jumped up and down at her daddy's side.

"I think mommy may have that for you."

Saylor nodded. "Sounds delicious," she smiled at him. "Thank you. Dinner all together is long overdue for us." Max knew she was referring to the last night they ate together as a family with Mia. The night Mia died. And Max had blamed Saylor for the accident ever since. Max nodded, and Saylor spoke again. "Speaking of all of us — is Sammy in his room?"

"Um, no. Brittany stopped by, looking for him. She convinced him to take a walk on the beach."

"Who's Brittany?" Saylor initially asked, but really she wanted to blurt out how unbelievable it was to know that Sammy was back on the beach. It was definitely the first step toward healing. And Saylor was grateful to *this girl named Brittany*, even though she didn't personally know her.

If Things Were Different

"A girl in his summer hang-out group, I guess. I assumed he knew her from the beach?" Max was a little uncertain of who Brittany was as well.

"My guess is she's the girl in the blue bikini that your son has his eye on," Saylor winked, and Max chuckled. "I am grateful to her for coming here and dragging him out of this cottage."

Max nodded. "It didn't look like she had to drag him."

Saylor laughed, but quickly turned serious. "I hope his first time out there isn't too emotional for him."

"Saylor, he's with a girl. He will hold it together." Max didn't seem worried. "He's not surfing, he's just getting his toes in the sand again."

"Do you think he will ever surf again?" Saylor looked glum.

"Eventually, yeah," Max stated. "It's just going to take awhile. I think we all need time to process this tragedy. I'm really concerned about Nash. He doesn't seem to want to talk."

Saylor looked down at her flip flops on her feet on the barnwood flooring for a moment. If she told her husband the truth, that she reached out to Nash, and was alone at a bar all afternoon with him, he would lose his mind. He would never understand her need to be there for him after his entire world fell apart. "Keep trying," she said. "I'm sure he's devastated."

"I hope he and Londyn are able to come together in their grief," Max said, still wanting to talk about Nash — and Saylor was ready to change the subject. For days, she wanted to talk to Max about all of the sadness and unfairness that had bombarded their lives, and he had shut her out. His timing was off now. And she didn't want to discuss Nash and Londyn rebuilding their relationship. She thought of kissing him. *That never should have happened.* This frazzled her in front of Max.

"Are we eating soon?" she blurted out.

"I can start the grill," Max said, looking a bit confused. "Are you okay?"

"Yeah, why?"

"Well I know you're not okay, none of us are, but you just seem edgy."

"I'm hungry." That was the first believable excuse she could think of at the moment.

"You do get cranky when your tummy is empty. I'll get going," Max chuckled, backing up to the refrigerator to retrieve the swordfish for the grill.

✽

If Things Were Different

Nash went home after he and Saylor parted ways from The Waterfront Bar. On the white sofa in their massive living room, Londyn heard him close the front door to their condo. She was curled up, with an afghan thrown over her legs. There was no noise in that room. The flat-screen television mounted high on the wall was dark. The music she had always played over their surround-sound system was silenced. She stared at the fireless fireplace. It was too hot outside to start a fire, but Londyn actually had contemplated doing so. She was chilled. Her body needed nourishment. She hadn't eaten much of anything in days, and she only drank hot tea all day long. Londyn was sad and isolated. Even with Nash living in the same house, she felt alone.

"Hi," he said, surprised to see her awake. Most times lately, she was asleep on that sofa when he came home. Or maybe she had pretended to be? It didn't really matter whichever way to either of them. They were no help to each other right now. They had both suffered the same devastating loss, but finding a common ground seemed impossible.

"Hello," she said back to him.

He wanted to ask if she had eaten anything, knowing he should push her to eventually or he would find her passed out from malnutrition.

She wondered where he had been most of the day again, and if he was spending his time alone like her. And when had he planned on returning to work? Without modeling on her agenda this summer, Londyn wouldn't be.

Nash started to walk out of the room, but he turned back. "How long are we going to live like this?" His question threw her, and for a moment she didn't have an answer for him.

And then she realized she did have something to say to him. "Live? You call this living? I'm stuck in limbo without Mia — and I don't ever see my way out. I don't want to live without her."

Nash slowly nodded his head. He also felt the same hopelessness that his wife spoke of, but he couldn't bring himself to tell her that. They never could communicate well. They were bonded only because of their daughter. And now she was gone. *So where did that leave the two of them, and their marriage?* "I need to get back to work. I feel like that might help, at least to busy my mind. Maybe you should, too?"

"Doing what? This model approaching forty years old has red, puffy eyes, and a pained face," Londyn didn't want to help herself to recover. Not now. Not yet. Maybe not ever. She only wanted to sink deeper into her grief. She missed Mia so badly that she physically ached for her daughter's presence. To see her again. To hear her voice. To hold her in her arms one more time. The finality of this devastation was driving Londyn out of her mind.

"Give yourself time then, Londyn. Eventually, we will both make it through this sadness." Nash heard his own words, and he was a bit taken aback. Just hours ago, he was ready to give up this useless fight as well. It was Saylor who had given him the will to survive, moment by moment. He wanted to feel stronger. He wanted to eventually move past the heart-wrenching pain of being a grieving parent. And he had Saylor to credit for saving him from the edge. Nash walked out of the room then, and upstairs to the bedroom that he and Londyn no longer shared. Lately, she had stayed on the couch throughout the daytime, and all night long.

He took out his cell phone from the pocket of his shorts. He knew he couldn't call her, because she was with her family. So he sent Saylor a text message instead.

I need a favor. And you're probably not going to like it. Londyn needs help. Will you try to reach her?

11

What he was asking of her was too much. It was absolutely ridiculous for Nash to think that Londyn would ever listen, much less open up, to her. From Londyn's perspective, Saylor was indirectly to blame for Mia's death. Saylor had blamed herself enough because she allowed the kids to surf together, knowing Mia wasn't as experienced as Sammy.

Saylor's reply to Nash was respectful, but honest.

This is a bad idea all-around. I'm the last person who can help her.

Nash was persistent.

I can't talk to her. She may be angry with you at first, but I know eventually she will listen. Will you just try? Please.

Saylor gave in. She didn't want to. But she did.

I'll stop by in the morning.

If Things Were Different

※

The next morning, Saylor sat on the front porch, rocking. She sipped her coffee out there before everyone else was awake. She was thinking about what she had agreed to do today, and how she was going to handle seeing Londyn.

Saylor remembered her final night with Mia, when she had some sort of an epiphany. She unexpectedly opened her eyes then to the fact that Londyn had tried terribly hard to mesh with them, as a family, and especially with Saylor as a friend. They were a family that Nash and Mia so effortlessly had always been a part of. Saylor felt a little pang of guilt in her chest again, just like she did that night when she was watching and listening to Mia speak of how important they all were to her, and to each other. For Mia, for that sweet girl's memory, Saylor would try to reach Londyn. She wondered if she should speak to Nash about giving his marriage another try. She sincerely hoped he would. But first, she had to start to with Londyn. And this was the day to try.

Max walked out, onto the front porch, dressed in flat front, pressed khakis and a red polo shirt with the M&N Solar Energy logo across the his left breast. "What brings you out here so early?"

"Thinking," she answered. "Nash texted me last night. Londyn isn't coping very well. He asked me to talk to her."

"You? Of all people? Nash obviously isn't thinking very clearly either," Max stated, and Saylor tried to ignore that he sounded snarky.

"Did you know that he's coming back to work today?" Saylor asked him, hoping Max already knew that information, or she would feel forced to explain why she had been talking to Nash so much.

"Yes, he told me," Max replied. "I think it will be good for him to attempt as much normalcy as he can again in his life. Work will definitely keep him busy."

"That's exactly his concern about Londyn. She has nothing to do, nothing else to busy her mind," Saylor stated.

"Are you really going over there?" Max asked her. He was concerned that the two of them would get into some terrible argument — or catfight. There had not been a mutual admiration between the two of them. Sure, Londyn tried, but she never seemed sincere either. And Max knew that Saylor never cared for the other woman. *Pun intended.*

"I told Nash that I would," Saylor said, taking another sip of her coffee.

"Well, good luck. I really don't know how you are going to handle her. She blames you for what happened."

"You did, too," Saylor bluntly added, "but you came around. Right?"

Max stared at her for a moment. "I'm sure there are things I've done that you've wished I had thought over first. I

If Things Were Different

honestly think a part of me will always believe that you could have had better control over those kids that night."

"I could have prevented Mia's death, huh?" Saylor felt anger rise in her chest, for her husband. She wanted to throw something at him, but her only option right now was hot coffee. She wasn't that cruel. "I loved that girl. I would have done anything to protect her. And if you don't believe me, then you don't know me at all."

Max halfheartedly nodded. "I'm going to be late for a meeting. Let me know how it goes."

Sometimes, Saylor had to stop herself from talking, from getting in that last sarcastic word. She purposely stayed silent. She clenched her jaw. And then under her breath, she mumbled, *son of a bitch,* as her husband walked off.

✱

Nash told her that the front door would be unlocked if Londyn didn't answer a knock or the doorbell. So after two rings and one hard knock, Saylor turned the door handle.

"Londyn?" she called out immediately when she stepped through the doorway. She was invading someone else's home and personal space. She didn't like how uncomfortable that felt. No answer came. And when Saylor took a few steps from the door, to peer around a half wall that separated the foyer and the living room, she saw Londyn, curled up and covered up, on one of the two white sofas.

"I don't want you here," Londyn spoke what sounded almost eerie and had the potential to echo in a quiet room with at least a twenty-foot high arched ceiling.

"I know that," Saylor responded, as she took the steps to enter that massive area. "I'm here anyway."

"Typical." Londyn muttered, and Saylor addressed her comment.

"Of me? Why? Because I'm concerned about you?"

"Save the pity party. You've just got some guilt strapped on your back that's weighing you down. It'll pass eventually. You have your children with you, safe and sound — and alive." That one stung, but Saylor kept moving toward the white sofa, opposite of the one Londyn was lying on. She sat down without invitation.

"I do feel guilty," Saylor began. "I could have sent Mia home early that night. I should have attempted to parent her like she wasn't a responsible young adult who was always in control of any situation."

"It was a stupid move," Londyn interrupted.

"On my part? Yeah, I guess it was." Saylor gave her that one. Londyn and Max seemed to share that popular opinion.

"My daughter was smarter than that," Londyn spoke, clarifying, and Saylor allowed her to continue. Londyn needed to talk this out, even if it was to verbally continue to place blame. *Anything. Just to feel some emotion again.* "I never had to worry about her making bad decisions, or going off to do something half-assed like we did as teenagers and even later as college students." Londyn was being not so lady-like right now. This was new for Saylor to witness. *But, Jesus. The woman was grieving. Let her curse if that's what she needed to do.*

Saylor smiled a little. She remembered their conversation that night at the cottage, and how Mia wanted to *live a little.* "I hear you," Saylor told Londyn. "We've all been there."

"I'm probably being naïve. Kids go away to college all of the time and do things that their parents never know of." Saylor was watching Londyn speak. She didn't have a drop of makeup on. Her long dark hair hung loose and wavy all over her head. She wore a white tank top, sans a bra, and the black leggings that were partially underneath her afghan were simple and comfortable. That was not a look that Saylor was familiar with seeing on Londyn. Even with a makeup-free face, and lounge clothing, and sadness in her red, puffy eyes — Saylor still saw Londyn's unmistakable beauty.

"I think you had a really good girl," Saylor began, hoping the two of them could continue to have a civil conversation. They were suddenly off to a good start. "It's obvious how hard she worked to attain what she did in only her first year of college, when others her age were there to be free and have a good time. She did mention that her roommate partied a lot…"

Londyn slightly giggled. The genuine life in her eyes at that moment warmed Saylor's heart. "Sally's a piece of work. I was concerned about that pairing at the start, but Mia didn't seem fazed by her wild ways."

"I'll share with you, what she said that night, if you want me to?" Saylor asked, and she watched Londyn sit up at little straighter on the end of the sofa.

"She wore her swimsuit underneath her clothes during dinner, in case she and Sammy or Syd would want to go for a swim. Sammy had talked about going surfing," Saylor paused, wondering to herself if her boy would ever face his grief and return to the water to conquer those waves, "Mia said she needed to learn to live it up more when she could, when the moments were staring her in the face. She talked about how college her first year was intense and mostly serious for her. She said she was not there to party like so many of her friends — like her roommate." Londyn listened raptly. This was a realization for her. These were moments that she wanted to hold onto now. Moments of her daughter's life, specific things that happened, words that her daughter had spoken, that she had not known about. No matter how painful it was going to be to hear what Saylor had to say, Londyn wanted to listen. A part of her was disgusted with herself right now for allowing her anger toward Saylor to begin to diminish. *She didn't want to need her like this. She should hate her. She wanted to. But she didn't. She never had.*

"Sammy was going surfing that night," Saylor continued. "It was his thing. Mia wanted to let loose and enjoy the moment, some time on the water, before she had to get back. I thought about how she was too young to be saddled with being a responsible adult already, all of the time. Of course, she studied hard and had lofty goals — and everyone was so proud of her for that. It was just nice to see her want to have a little fun." Saylor choked up as she finished speaking. "If I had known... Oh God, Londyn, if only I had just stopped her—"

Londyn bent her body forward, and cried in her open palms. She completely covered her face, and sobbed. Saylor sat across from her, on her own separate sofa, silently allowing her own tears to freefall. She never got up. She couldn't physically reach for her. It's not who they were as women. *Had they ever really been friends? Saylor wondered if circumstance had not brought the two of them together as it had, could they have cared about each other in another time or another place, if things were different?*

When the tears ceased, Londyn spoke first. "When you walked in here, uninvited, I wanted to muster up the strength to throw you out. I'm just going to say it, I don't like you." Londyn never said *hate*. A reference to *dislike* was much milder. "I may have come across as friendly and cordial all of these years as we've appeased our husbands, and I've also allowed my daughter to be so connected to your family — but I just don't care about you. Am I a bitch for that? Well, if I am, so are you."

Saylor's eyes widened. She actually wanted to laugh. This was the first time, ever, that she and Londyn Parker had been in sync. "I am," Saylor chimed in. "I saw how hard you've tried to be my friend. I had no interest in swapping secrets and giggling with you. You are the woman who turned my life upside down when I was nineteen years old and completely in love with a man that I wanted to spend the rest of forever with. So, yeah, I get it. I understand. It's a relief to stop pretending, isn't it?"

"Fuck yes!" Londyn replied, and Saylor belted out a laugh.

Saylor believed that Londyn was going to be okay. Yes, she was a woman who was drowning in her grief on her sofa for days on end. *So what? If she needed to do that, for however long it took, she should. She certainly had every right.* But, once the tears subsided and she was ready to pick herself up, this was a woman strong enough to carry on. She may not realize it, Nash may not be able to see it, but Saylor did.

"Do you want me to go now?" Saylor spoke, directly and honestly. She would report back to Nash that his wife was not a weakling. She would never be the same, no. But she would eventually make do, and get by, and be okay.

"Not really," Londyn heard herself reply, "but I understand if you have to leave."

"Maybe I could come back sometime? Or, we could get you out of here for lunch? If or when you're ready?" All of this, the words they were swapping, dumfounded both of them. Saylor awaited a response.

"I'd like that," Londyn smiled. And her expression wasn't faked or forced.

12

Saylor's message to Nash, as soon as she drove away from the condo, was short and surprising.

That went amazingly well.

His response was almost immediate.

Can I call you?

Yes, but I'm driving so I'll put you on speaker.

Saylor answered on the first ring.

"You're kidding me, right?" Nash asked her. "The woman I left on the couch this morning was distraught and distant as she's been for several days."

"She was that," Saylor agreed, "at first. She never answered the door, and she wasn't at all happy that I let myself in and then ignored her requests for me to leave."

"So what changed?" Nash asked, feeling impatient.

"I'm not exactly sure. We just started talking, and crying. I was open and honest with her. I told her what happened that night, the things Mia talked about, and how free she wanted to feel in the moment because she worked so hard studying all of the time. Londyn really seemed to want to know what I had to say. Nash, she's much stronger than you give her credit for."

"Unbelievable," he spoke.

"Just give her some time, and be there for her, and let her hold you up as well. The two of you have a shared pain, and you can get through this together." Saylor thought she had made a wonderful assumption, but Nash crushed it.

"Saylor, I'm leaving her. My marriage is over. Your reassurance that she's strong just means that I don't have to wait this out." Nash sounded as if he was speaking of a business deal — not a woman he had been married to for almost two decades — and Saylor was disgusted.

"You're an asshole if you walk out on her now," Saylor stated, plain and simple, and she ended their call. She also ignored his call back. He never left her a voicemail, but he did send a text to her a few minutes later.

Londyn and I are finished, but you and I are not.

If Things Were Different

Saylor deleted his text immediately. The last thing she needed was for one of her children, or Max, to intercept that private message to her from Nash.

※

Nash made it back to the condo around dinner time, but there was no plan to eat anything. He lacked an appetite anyway, considering his first day back to work was emotionally draining. Either people completely ignored the fact that his daughter died, or that was all they wanted to talk about with him. *I'm so sorry about your daughter...* rang in his ears. He was sorry too. Damn sorry that this pain had a way of catching up to him when he was coasting along and doing pretty well. It stopped him too abruptly every time. Like a slap in the face or a punch in the gut, the pain would return, and Nash would realize that he would never again see her face — or receive that daily text or phone call from his daughter. He couldn't bring himself to delete her number from his phone. Not yet. Probably not ever.

The living room was empty. The sofa, that Londyn had camped out on for days, was put back together with multi-colored decorative throw pillows tossed on it. *Had Saylor been right? Was Londyn strong enough and ready to attempt getting back into the land of living?* Ready or not, Nash was looking to face another big change in his life. Life without both his daughter, and his wife.

Nash went upstairs, en route to his bedroom, but before he made it there, he saw that the door to Mia's room was wide open. Londyn had shut it the night they returned from the tragedy at the beach, and neither one of them had any desire to open it and go inside. Nash once heard that sometimes it takes people a full year, or longer, to sift through the belongings of a lost loved one. He really didn't feel up to going into Mia's room tonight, but that's where he found Londyn when he hesitantly stepped through the open doorway.

She was sitting with her legs crisscrossed on the floor, near their daughter's bed. The bedding, neatly made the morning after the last night's sleep Mia had on this earth, had a few outfits strewn across it. That's what Mia did before she went out somewhere. Anyone who lived with her knew that she was indecisive about her clothing most times. She would try on two or three things before she chose one to wear.

Londyn looked up at Nash, and saw him staring at the bed. "I used to tell her all the time to hang her clothes back up in the closet after she decided against wearing something," Londyn stated, from down on the floor. Her voice sounded raspy, as if she had been crying too much.

Nash nodded his head. "I know, I remember. It's too hard to be in here right now... why are you doing this already?"

"There are no dos and don'ts with this, are there?" Londyn asked him, making a valid point. "I feel close to her in here. It still smells like her. These are the things she last touched, and wore. I'm not in here to pack up anything. A part of me doesn't even want to move a thing, ever."

If Things Were Different

"Do you want to know what I hate most about this pain?" Nash asked her, and Londyn nodded her head. "Just when you think you've got a handle on it, you're doing better and feeling stronger, something will hit you, and you fucking crumble." Right now was one of those times for Nash.

Londyn held her hand over her mouth and suppressed a sob. This was the most honest and open that her husband had been with her since they lost their daughter.

"I may not yet be exactly where you are on this grief train, but I hear you. I'm off the couch. I've showered. I actually spoke to someone today, other than myself — and it felt good." Nash listened, and of course he knew she meant Saylor.

"Was someone here, or did you go out?" Nash played along. The last thing he wanted was for Londyn to know that he had sent Saylor.

"Saylor stopped by."

Nash widened his eyes on purpose. "I hope you didn't try to throw her out."

"At first, I definitely wanted to," Londyn admitted, "but then I gave in and listened to what she came to say." Nash waited for her to go on. He was afraid that saying something, anything, in Saylor's defense would put him under fire. "Saylor's in pain too. As much as it has unnerved me over the years, she loved Mia — her whole family did."

"Yeah, they sure did," Nash cleared his throat, "but no one is going to miss her the way we will."

Londyn blinked free a few tears and that fell onto her cheeks. "God yes," she replied. "Do you want to know my biggest fear?"

Nash said, "Yeah…I do," as he walked further into his daughter's bedroom and bent down to his knees on the floor. He didn't get overly close to Londyn, but he faced her directly.

"What if there's a fire here and all of her pictures, those prints of her growing up, are destroyed? What if our phones crash and our photographs are deleted? I don't want to," Londyn choked on a sob before she continued again, "forget what our little girl looked like, then and now. I'm afraid my mind will lose those details of those precious features she had on her face…and those sporadic freckles she had on her pale shoulders from getting sunburned as a kid. Remember when we took her on that Disney cruise when she was five? I was so mad at you because I thought you had put sunscreen on her, but you hadn't protected her skin."

"And I was sure that you had…" Nash added. The two of them stopped speaking and only looked at each other for a moment. Londyn was thinking how there was no one else in the world who could share those memories of Mia with her, not the way that Nash could. And Nash was thinking that there was absolutely no way he could ask his wife for a divorce tonight. It was too soon. He did have a compassionate heart, and what surprised him most at this moment was he hadn't felt this connected to Londyn in a very long time. If ever. And then he said, "We will make copies of all the photos and keep them in a safe deposit box, and I'll be sure to frequently back up our phones, too."

If Things Were Different

"Thank you," Londyn wiped the tears from her face with her fingers. She was touched, and reassured that her memories of Mia would be protected and preserved.

"You have to do me a favor too," Nash told her. "Tell me more things like that when they cross your mind. Like her freckled shoulders…"

Londyn smiled through more of her tears.

13

Saylor couldn't sleep. She often envied Max for how quickly he could fall asleep, and stay asleep all night long until his alarm sounded and forced him to peel his eyes. As she often did, Saylor got out of bed and went outside. Her trusty yellow rocking chair awaited her anytime she needed it. She looked for constants like that in her life.

The night air was dark and quiet. She could hear the ocean from where she sat. It was a magical sound for her, as it had always been since she was a child. Her father was an avid sailor, hence the name of his only child. She missed him. His laugh, the way that he threw his head back. His wisdom, how he had told her to follow her heart and it would lead her to happiness.

If Things Were Different

"Take good care of Mia up there, dad," Saylor spoke out into the night. "I don't understand why bad things have to happen to good people. She was one of the best." Saylor sat quiet for awhile. The air was warm, as she wore only a white v-neck t-shirt with a pocket over the left breast, and aqua blue panties. She giggled at how her polished toenails matched her undies.

Staring out into the distance forced Saylor to sit up straighter, and focus her eyes a little harder. She thought she saw movement along the shore. A tall, broad figure. A man with a bit of a swagger that she'd spot anywhere. In a crowd. In the dark of night. She thought of staying still, and letting him pass by. She had no outside porch lights on. *Why draw attention to herself?*

Even still, she reached for her cell phone which she had brought with her out there. She, like everyone else in the world, was attached to that darn thing. Like a lifeline.

It was almost one a.m., but she was awake and out there and so was he, so Saylor sent him a short text.

Wait up.

After Nash pulled out his phone from the pocket of his shorts, he read the text, and he stopped walking. He knew that he was in close proximity to the cottage. He looked that way while he walked, but it was dark and he obviously had not seen anyone. But Saylor had spotted him. He waited in place, his flip flops sunk in the sand. The water washed to shore a few times before he could see how close she was, coming toward him. Her boxy white t-shirt in the moonlight sent a warm feeling through him. It was the simplest things about her that made her incredibly sexy. She wasn't high maintenance. She was chic. She was a tomboy at times. And she was both pretty and cute wrapped up into one little hot body.

When Saylor reached him, she spoke first. "You're a little ways from home in the middle of the night."

"I do this sometimes. I'm able to find a little peace out here since—"

"I know, me too," Saylor stated, sighing. Missing Mia was overwhelming them. And learning to cope was going to be a long road full of both weak and strong moments.

"I can see your underwear," Nash unexpectedly mentioned, as he purposely tried to break through their sadness.

Saylor laughed out loud. "What are you, five?"

Nash laughed at her. "I don't feel like a kid when I look at you…" She wasn't wearing a bra underneath that t-shirt.

"Alright, alright," Saylor scolded him. "Who cares? You've seen me in less anyway."

"Are you always such a flirt in the middle of the night?" he asked her.

"Only with loners on the beach." They both laughed. "How's Londyn? Any better?" Saylor switched back to serious mode with him.

"She's dealing, she really is," Nash answered. "You were right. She's a tough cookie."

If Things Were Different

"Are you really going to leave her? Please don't. Not now. Not yet, at least." Saylor practically begged him.

"Not yet," he agreed.

"Good," Saylor's voice gave away her relief.

"But is it really fair to her for me to stay? She deserves better."

"You married her when you didn't have to. You were the best daddy to your baby, right alongside of her. I'd say Londyn got someone pretty deserving for a young woman who could have ended up raising a child alone. And besides, she's a beautiful woman."

"She's not you," Nash replied.

Saylor stayed silent for a moment. "Max and my children are my life now. I'm not unhappy here. I live on the beach, for the love of God."

"We were just getting started," Nash said, referring to their time together many years ago.

"Yeah I know, and it was hardly long enough," Saylor added, honestly.

"I think about what I could have done different," Nash told her, "and there have been times in my life when I wish I had committed to being a father to Mia, but not a husband to Londyn. But now that she's gone, I have no regrets because I gave her two parents, a real family for as long as she was here." He cleared his throat and looked down at the sand. Saylor reached for him. She touched his arm. Standing that close to the water, she could feel a mist on his skin.

"That was beautifully said," Saylor began, "and I completely agree with you now. Mia deserved the best life, and it was you who made sure she got it."

"So no regrets?" he clarified, as there had been so many times throughout the years that he believed Saylor hated him for the choice he made to leave her.

"No..." Saylor replied, and she pulled her hand away from touching his arm.

"So now what do we do? I see this second chance hanging in the balance. And I feel like if we do not follow our hearts, we will have something to regret for the rest of our lives. We could have a life together, Saylor. A happy one. The one we were supposed to have."

Saylor thought of her father. *Follow your heart and it will lead you to happiness.* This was hard. *Why was life so difficult?* Being with Nash, like this, was effortless, but the final choice to truly be with him would tear apart lives and hurt too many people that they loved.

"One of us has to keep a clear head in this," she told him, and obviously it was going to have to be her.

Before she could say more, he spoke again. "I remember when you used to like a little clouded judgment." She smiled at his words. She recalled the nights they drank beer on the waterfront, underage and feeling free. Riding on the back of a motorcycle with him, helmet free and relishing the wind in her long blonde hair at that time. Sex on the beach with him. She had not forgotten what it felt like to be high on love. His love. "You haven't changed at all," he told her as he watched her face, and knew she remembered everything about the two of them.

She laughed a little. "Look closer," she stated, implying that she had crow's feet and laugh lines and sun damage.

"If I get any closer, I'm going to kiss you," he stated as a matter of fact.

Saylor never moved, but she should have backed up from him. She knew she should have. He reached out his arms and took both of her hands in his. He watched her close her eyes for a moment. And then he pulled her against him. Close. He could feel her bare chest — under the thin, practically iridescent material of her t-shirt— against him.

He never made the move to kiss her. He only held her, as she extended her arms around him and tightened her grip. And when they finally pulled apart, he had a proposition for her.

"Go away with me…"

"What?" Saylor believed him to be completely crazy.

"Just one weekend. I'll tell Londyn it's business. You can tell Max the same."

"I don't travel for grant work," she stated.

"Come up with something," he said, realizing she had not refused his offer.

"I don't know if I can do this, Nash," Saylor sighed, and she felt a strange, nervous energy overtake her body.

"Two days together," he propositioned. "And after, you can choose to return to your life as you know it, or begin one with me."

This time Saylor did back away. She stumbled in the sand twice as she made her escape from him and back to the cottage, to the home she shared with her husband and children. And each time she turned around and looked back at Nash, still standing on the shore, she questioned and she marveled if she could really do what he was asking. And what terrified her most was that she wanted to.

14

You are out of your mind! Saylor chided herself. There was no way she could fall asleep now, but she slipped back into bed anyway next to Max. He never stirred. And for some reason that annoyed her right now. After sharing a life together for fifteen years, everything had become predictable, routine, and oftentimes mundane. She could expect to get out of bed in the middle of the night, and not once had her husband ever noticed or tiptoed through the cottage to check on her. She wasn't even certain that he knew she habitually sat on the porch alone in the middle of the night. She didn't want to allow herself to compare Max with Nash, but she went there anyway in her thoughts. Nash was unpredictable and exciting. He relished in spur of the moment plans. A beer in the middle of the day at a bar on the waterfront. A walk in the dark along the shore. Pack a bag for a getaway. That was his proposition to her.

Insanity. She would have to lie to her husband and children. And then what? Cheat on Max too? That's not who Saylor was. She had integrity and values, and respect for her husband and their marriage. She thought of her and Nash, and their shared kiss on the dock at the bar. And how just moments ago he held her in his arms on the beach. There was an undeniable connection between them. Not to mention their chemistry. *The explosive sexual attraction.* They had done so well at respecting those boundaries for years. Too much had changed too fast lately. Saylor recognized that Nash was vulnerable in his state of grief. His only mindset was — the time to live is now or never. He had a valid point. But Saylor had a family to protect, to keep intact. She needed to stay away from him. No more daytime secret meetings at bars floating on water, or moonlight strolls along the shore. Both of those reunions occurred because Saylor was the initiator. She had texted him twice. All she had to do was reach out to him, and Nash in turn wanted her close. It was time to get back to keeping him at arm's length, because when he was any closer, Saylor wanted him. But she told herself, lying next to Max in their dark bedroom, that if she carelessly gave in to her old desire, it would cost her everything.

*

If Things Were Different

Londyn stood in front of the window that spanned the entire wall of the condo's sunroom. She peered out into their backyard. A thunderstorm distorted her view through the glass, but she could see that one-hundred-feet-tall white oak tree at the perimeter of the yard. The wind and rain were beating it, mercilessly. It didn't matter though, because when the storm passed, that massive, indestructible tree — which was every bit of fifty inches in diameter — would stand tall again with its straight trunk and broad, rounded crown. Mia used to call it their miracle tree, because it had wondrously survived two lightning strikes in the last decade. No one could explain it, but the tree had not died, not even in parts after lightning struck it. Other than several burned and broken branches on the ground, following both lightning strikes that were witnessed by them once and a neighbor the second time, there were no burns or obvious signs of trauma to the tree. It remained healthy, and not the least bit weakened or susceptible to disease. The tree carried on, Londyn thought. How symbolic was that in relation to the way she felt now. She had been struck in the worst possible way. Her daughter was gone. But she had to stand tall and carry on. Nash was doing it. *So why couldn't she?*

She contemplated calling Saylor. She needed to get out of that condo. Some adult interaction might do her some good. After the storm passed.

✱

The beach in front of the cottage functioned as a buffer, as protection to the residents living near the ocean. That beach safeguarded homes from the high winds and waves of a powerful storm. Sammy was in his bedroom, and Saylor had appeased Syd with a board game. She was setting up the pieces to play another round, when Saylor stood up and peered out of the outer glass door on the front of their cottage. Funny that it was actually called a *storm door* for protection in bad weather. Saylor always loved to watch it storm on the beach. She was more intrigued than frightened. She feared a little for their safety while feeling drawn to view more of that disturbance of the atmosphere. Max preferred to shut the cottage down during a storm, as he would make a point to close both of the front doors and all the window blinds. He was at work now, so Saylor eyed the wind and rain through the glass door that separated her from it.

"I'm ready for another game, mommy," Saylor heard Syd say.

She turned away from the storm door for only a second, because she wanted to watch more, perhaps until it completely passed. Her children were not at all afraid of storms. Saylor really had not made the effort to teach them not to be, they had just learned from her calm and curious reactions. Neither one of them were as intrigued by a loud wind and rain thrashing thunderstorm as Saylor though.

After the calm, three hours later, another storm was brewing. Syd had fallen asleep on the sofa, and Sammy was still closed up in his bedroom, but this time he had three of his friends in there with him. Two boys, and the other was Brittany.

If Things Were Different

Saylor stood outside on the front porch, staring at the sky and those dark clouds that had formed in the distance. She hadn't been very productive today, as she and her kids stayed inside. She needed to catch up on some of her grant work, but hadn't been able to really concentrate in weeks actually. Since she wasn't sleeping well, Saylor decided she would attempt to write tonight. In mid thought, her cell phone rang behind her. She retrieved it from one of the yellow rocking chairs. *Londyn was calling her.*

"Londyn…hi," Saylor answered, stopping herself before she also said, *how are you?* With tragedy so raw in her life yet, the last question she should be expected to answer was how she was coping with the unfairness that life hurled at her.

"Hi. Am I interrupting anything?" Londyn asked.

"Nope, just storm watching today. It looks like there's another one coming." Weather was always a safe topic with anyone. It wasn't as if she and Londyn were strangers, but they never contacted each other like this — per an unexpected phone call as if they were close friends.

"I know, I was hoping the next one would miss us," Londyn spoke. "Would you want to take a drive, grab a bite to eat, or have a drink with me? After the threat of the storm passes, of course." Saylor remained quiet on her end, waiting for Londyn to elaborate. And when Saylor realized that Londyn was not going to speak anything else until she replied with some sort of an answer, she quickly spoke up.

"Oh, um, yeah sure," she began. "Are you having a difficult day?" *How else was she supposed to ask her what made her reach out like this?*

"I just need to get out of this house. Nash is working, and I don't know how much comfort he would be to me anyway. This is awkward, I know, and let me just say it to get it out of the way. You and I… we don't extend invitations to each other like this. We don't reach out. I just didn't know who else to call," Londyn paused. Saylor winced for a moment. It's not that she cringed, she just felt the awkwardness of this phone call. *Was Londyn looking for comfort*? Saylor knew this could not have been easy for her. To reach out. To say that she needed *a friend*. And she was right to imply that they weren't friends. Or at least not close ones. But that didn't matter right now. If Londyn needed someone to talk to, Saylor would be there for her.

"I'll come by for you, and we'll go from there. Dress casual, or whatever you're wearing now in the house today is fine. I'm wearing cut-offs and a tank top," Saylor laughed a little.

"I'm in what I call my uniform lately… leggings and a tank," Londyn stated, and such a simple conversation felt effortless between them. All they were talking about was clothing. Londyn had spent so many years trying too hard with Saylor, and never once having a single thing in common with her.

"Perfect!" Saylor replied. "See you in about fifteen or twenty minutes."

If Things Were Different

Saylor looked at the sky again before she stepped back inside. *That storm could miss them,* she thought.

She wanted to call for Sammy to come out of his room, but Syd was still napping on the sofa, so she went to his door and knocked twice. His friends were in there still, and she wanted to respect their privacy. But now she expected Sammy to hang out with his little sister once she woke up.

Sammy opened the door, and Saylor attempted to step inside. He didn't move back, so she couldn't get in. "What are you doing?" she asked him, pushing the door in his direction.

"Nothing," he replied, and he looked caught. Saylor glanced past him and saw Brittany sitting on the foot end of Sammy's bed. She managed to look around the rest of the room, and no one else was in there.

"Where are the guys?" Saylor asked him, knowing exactly why her son had looked caught off guard. *Or almost caught in the act?*

"They did a window escape earlier."

Well at least her boy was honest, Saylor thought, but she nearly freaked out knowing that her teenage son was alone in his bedroom, probably on the bed, with a girl. Under her same roof. Max would flip out. As if Saylor had not already been on his irresponsible list as of late.

"Sam…" Saylor gave him a mother's *what the hell are you doing,* look. "It's time for Brittany to go, too. I need you to watch Syd for an hour or so. I have to run out."

"What? Why? She can stay, can't she? And it's going to storm again…can't your errand wait?" All at once, her son had sounded like he wanted to grow up (and have a girl stay with him, alone at the cottage) and then he turned around and acted as if he didn't want his mommy to leave the house in case of a storm.

"She can stay if the two of you spend your time in the kitchen or living room. I mean it, Sammy. Syd will be awake soon. Babysit." *Don't make a baby*, she wanted to add.

"We will," Sammy spoke up, and Sydney noticed that Brittany looked a little embarrassed, *at what Mrs. Bach had implied they were doing…or about to do.*

"Don't make me regret this," Saylor warned, as she backed through the doorway. And leaving suddenly felt like a bad idea all around. Another storm was coming. She was leaving her children home alone. Sammy had a girlfriend.

But Londyn needed her.

15

The storm hit Morehead City when Saylor was just a few miles away from Londyn and Nash's condo. She could barely see through the windshield as the wind was thrashing the rain sideways. Saylor already decided that she and Londyn were going to stay sheltered for awhile once she made it there. Driving to a restaurant or bar was not urgent in a major thunderstorm.

*

Nash pulled into their three-car garage. It pained him to see Mia's car in there, too. They would eventually have to sell it. It was just another one of those things that he and Londyn were in no hurry to part with. Getting rid of her things was too final too soon. He had driven home from work before the storm hit, and only had been caught in the brunt of it for the last mile or less. He left the office because Londyn had called him and asked him to come home. All she said was *it's important.*

When Nash made his way into the kitchen from the garage, Londyn was standing near the octagon table. Her Kate Spade handbag was on the tabletop, and Nash noticed three matching pieces of luggage at her feet.

"What's going on?" was the first thing he asked. She had not mentioned any modeling, or plans to travel somewhere. It wasn't unusual for Londyn to travel solo for her work, but the fact that she may be modeling again had taken Nash by surprise. She had also seemed over-packed for a gig.

"I signed on to model again," she began, and Nash nodded. He was actually proud of her for forcing herself back into the business. She was struggling with aging. And still reeling from a tragic loss. She could easily make legitimate excuses and give it all up.

"That's wonderful. Where are you headed?" Nash was sincerely curious.

"L.A.," she answered. "I'm on contract for at least a year with a new skincare line. I'm going to be the face of an anti-aging product. I guess being an *older* model isn't so bad after all." She smiled, and Nash chuckled. He thought how good it was to see her having a purpose again.

If Things Were Different

"That will mean a lot of travel for you then, huh?" Nash wasn't bothered by that in the least. He was never the type of husband who clung to her. He willingly encouraged her freedom. And over the years he had handled the single dad days with Mia exceptionally well.

"Nash, I'm leaving," Londyn stated as a matter of fact. She sounded sad, but determined as she spoke. Gone was the excitement to travel, to model again, which had been there a moment ago. "I am moving to California. I will come back when you decide what you want to do with the condo. I'll want to have my share of Mia's things." She just wasn't ready for that yet.

"Wait? You're leaving? As in leaving me, and our marriage?" Nash was floored. He honestly believed, the day they parted ways, that he would be the bad guy. The marriage destroyer.

Londyn nodded. "Yes. I don't know what you want to do about the divorce proceedings. I would like to get settled in LA first, and then hopefully we can agree to keep this amicable. I have no intention of taking you for a ride. We can joint file if you want? Just pick a lawyer for us."

Nash was dumbfounded. And he was nearly speechless. "This is what you really want?" he asked, knowing it was what he certainly wanted. But she was being so damn nice and cooperative that he felt the need to give her that in return.

"I think we both know there's nothing left for us." She didn't have to say it. Mia was gone. Their daughter was the tie that bonded them.

He wanted to wish her well. He wanted to at least drive her to the airport. But before he could offer anything, the doorbell rang.

"I'll get it," Londyn spoke as she made her way from the kitchen and through the living room. Nash followed her to see who was at the door during a thunderstorm.

Her clothes had been rained on, and her hair was damp as Saylor stepped into the foyer of the condo. She was taken aback by two things. Londyn was in dress clothes. She wore a sleeveless black button down blouse and fitted white pants, with black wedges that topped her off at six feet tall. And, Nash was there.

"Come in," Londyn invited her. "This rainstorm can stop anytime, right?"

Saylor nodded in agreement. "Oh tell me about it. I'm drenched, and underdressed too I see. I thought we agreed to stay casual?" Now Nash was confused. He never spoke to her, and Saylor had only given him a fleeting glance.

"That's because you and I are not going anywhere," Londyn started to explain, as she led both Saylor and Nash into the massive living room. No one sat down. The awkward feeling in the room among all three of them kept them from making themselves more comfortable and feeling at ease. "I asked you both to come here. Nash already knows that I'm leaving. He just got here a few minutes ago. My luggage is packed, and I'm flying out to California today." Saylor assumed for business, but she never spoke. "I'm moving there for a modeling job. And Nash and I are getting a divorce."

If Things Were Different

"I just heard of all of this literally five minutes ago," Nash finally spoke, and Saylor's eyes widened at him.

"I know I've sprung a lot on the both of you. I just need a fresh start. I'm not running away. I just want to begin again somewhere else, by myself." Londyn seemed incredibly content. Saylor and Nash had both picked up on that.

"I'm happy for you, I mean, the modeling part. You deserve that," Saylor spoke, feeling as if she was grasping to find the right words. "But I'm not even sure what I'm supposed to say about your divorce. I wish you two wouldn't make a rash decision like that so soon after losing Mia. Don't they say to never make any major life changes the first year of your grief?" Saylor was rambling, and feeling more awkward by the second. *Why had she summoned her there right now? This was between Londyn and Nash. A husband and wife. But time was now running out on that union.*

"It's amicable, right Nash?" Londyn looked at her husband.

"Yes, I mean we never even discussed it. You made the choice to leave and I'm not stopping you." Nash wasn't angry, he was simply speaking the truth. "But why did you ask Saylor here?" There. Nash had spoken exactly what was front and center on Saylor's mind.

Londyn stood across from the two of them. They were nearly shoulder to shoulder. Saylor thought she should move, but Londyn seemed to have them right where she wanted. She spoke to them as if she was the instructor and they were her apprentices.

"I think you both know why," Londyn began. "I was the reason the two of you parted ways nineteen years ago. I got in the way of a great love. I was pregnant, and Nash chose me and our baby." Saylor wondered why they needed to rehash that now. Nash seemed intrigued by what Londyn was doing, and saying. "And now, I want to be the one to bring the two of you back together."

This time Saylor stepped away from Nash. "This is insane!" she blurted out. "Hello? What about Max — my husband! And our children? You can't disregard the people I love like that."

"I'm not," Londyn attempted to defend herself. "I'm just stepping out of the way now. What happens once I'm gone will be what the two of you choose. That's what I'm telling you both. I am no longer a part of this equation. I am not angry or bitter. I'm just giving the two of you back to each other. Just be happy. I think it's quite obvious that there's still something powerful lingering between you. I don't want to see Max or your children get hurt. But I also don't want to stand in the way anymore."

The thunder cracked and Saylor jumped. She was on edge anyway. This was like some sort of ridiculous dream that she was going to wake up from any moment as she turned over on her sofa. Londyn was handing them back to each other? As if nothing or no one else mattered. It annoyed Saylor to hear Londyn speak so freely of their lives, and she was especially miffed at the expression Nash wore. He seemed intrigued and ready to jump in with two eager feet.

Saylor spoke to Londyn. "Just take some time for yourself, please, before you regret this. Rethink it. This isn't right."

"This is the most content I have felt about anything in a very long time, and it actually has nothing to do with losing Mia. Well maybe that has given me the clarity and the courage to do this, but I do mean I feel in my heart that this is *right* for me." Londyn stepped toward Saylor and took both of her hands in hers. "Friends. Us? Who knew? I am grateful that we finally reached this point. You drove in a storm today to rescue me because you thought I needed a friend. A friend," Londyn repeated. "Thank you."

Saylor felt her eyes tear up. "So stay! Be my friend! Let's build on that, and you and Nash can make your marriage work." Saylor knew that she was being unheard. By both of them. She wanted to scream and yell at how unfair this was to her. It was as if they were both pushing her to hurt her family. To give up on Max.

Londyn pulled her close and into a brief, meaningful embrace. "You will do what's best for you, I know that. Just be happy." And then Londyn turned to Nash. She held out her hand to him, and he reached in turn for hers. Saylor felt uncomfortably like a third wheel. She was about to witness their goodbye. The end of their era of being together.

They were of equal height as Londyn was wearing almost three-inch wedges. He pulled her into a tight embrace. And then Saylor heard their final parting words to each other.

"Take care of yourself," Londyn told him. Her voice was strong, and her eyes were dry.

"Goodbye beautiful…" Nash spoke back to her.

There was an Uber waiting outside on the driveway. The rain was still pouring down. Nash was concerned about Londyn's safety and well-being. He made a point to step ahead of her and immediately suggested he back out his vehicle to allow the Uber driver to pull into their garage so she and her things would not get soaked in the rain. Londyn accepted his offer, and he also carried her luggage out for her. All the while, Saylor waited alone in their massive living room. She paced. And then she stood still. Her mind was reeling. Nash walked back into the house and into that living room.

"I thought I would be the one to hurt her," he stated, shaking his head in disbelief. "She's really being unbelievable about all of this." Nash looked both relieved and satisfied. And again, Saylor was annoyed. The rain pounded on the condo's rooftop, and she raised her voice to be heard.

"How can you go along with this absurdity? She needs you! The last thing she can handle now is being alone."

"You heard her, she wanted to leave. She seemed pumped about this modeling job. She's going to be the face of a new anti-aging skincare line. This is what she needs to get out of that slump of growing older and feeling not worthy."

"Stop it!" Saylor demanded. "Just stop. Don't make small talk. And don't look at this as an opportunity for us. We can't, Nash. You love Max just as much as I do! I have children to think about, to put first." Saylor felt panicked. He was free. She was not. She knew he was going to pressure her, and she doubted her strength not to surrender to him.

Nash stepped closer to her. He touched her bare shoulders with his open palms. "Shhh… calm down. You don't have to do anything right now. I'm here. This time I am here, and I am not running off to do the right thing for someone else. Yes, I do love Max. But you're acting as if you've forgotten that he was second to me in your heart."

"Don't say that. Don't say those words." Saylor choked on a sob, and Nash pulled her close. She pushed her face into his chest and started to cry. "He's my husband," Saylor heard herself say. And yes, now more than ever before, she needed to remind herself of that. *She was committed to Max.*

The condo suddenly lost power. The storm, which was finally beginning to die down, had caused the outage. And now the two of them were stuck, alone and together in there, in the darkness.

16

A calm atmosphere followed the stormy weather, which was what Saylor witnessed as she shifted her jeep into park at the cottage and walked up the narrow cobblestone path.

She now had to morph into mom mode to check on the kids, and prep something for dinner. Max wasn't home yet, thank goodness, but she would tell him later where she had been this afternoon.

"Hey mom," Sammy was the first to greet her, and she questioned his cheerful mood from the sofa until she tuned in to her surroundings. Brittany and Syd were in the kitchen baking cookies, she guessed on that, as something delicious met her sense of smell in the doorway.

"Look at you," Saylor said, smiling at the girls. "I may not have a plan for dinner yet, but dessert is covered." It was easy to slip back into routine with her children. They couldn't read her, or see through her mask of disguise. Especially when they were wrapped up in a girlfriend and cookie baking. Max, rather, could sometimes be perceptive, so Saylor prepared herself for that later.

"Dad called while you were gone," Sammy said, instantly grabbing her attention. "He said you weren't answering your cell." So Max had called. Had he been worried about her and the kids' safety in the storm? Was he upset when he found out she left the kids home alone during threatening weather?

"Oh he did? Yeah, I left it in the jeep." That was the truth. "Did he want something?"

"Just checking on us, I think," Sammy stated. "He said the power went out in his building but the back-up generator kicked on." Saylor was well aware of the power outage in parts of the city.

"Did you lose power here too?" she asked, hoping not. Before she rushed out, she hadn't thought to be sure they knew where the flashlights and candles were stored.

"No," Sammy said, and then he was distracted by Brittany's giggle in the kitchen. She and Syd were acting silly, spooning cookie dough on the baking sheet. "Where did you go? The storm got really bad after you left."

It certainly did. Saylor had driven in it. "To see Londyn." Sammy nodded. He still couldn't talk much about what happened to Mia — and his involvement in it. His guilt pained him. And he really hoped Londyn was okay.

Saylor made her way down the hallway after telling all of them that she would be right back. She assumed Brittany wanted to stay for dinner, so they would talk about food in a few minutes. Right now, Saylor bent over the bathroom sink to splash water on her face. She needed a moment to regroup. The reflection in the mirror stared her down. *What have you done?* A pained expression took over her face.

✱

The kids talked her into ordering pizza. Saylor agreed, but she wanted to call Max first to find out when he was coming home for dinner. His cell phone rang enough times to send her call to his voicemail, which wasn't completely out of the ordinary for Max when he was working. Saylor never left him a message. Pizza wasn't urgent and he could always eat the leftovers. She was in the process of inquiring what pizza toppings Brittany liked (or did not like) when her cell phone rang. Saylor saw that it was Max.

"Hey honey, are you headed home soon?"

"Saylor! It's Penny." Max's secretary was calling her from his cell phone. Immediate panic rose in Saylor's chest. "I called an ambulance for Max. I'm not sure what's wrong, it could just be anxiety — or his heart."

"Oh God, okay, I'm on my way!" Saylor spoke into the phone, as she glanced at all three of the children in her house, staring at her with panicked faces. *Something was wrong with Max.* Too many thoughts raced through her mind.

Where she had been this afternoon. Max's missed phone call to her. Had he wanted to tell her that the wasn't feeling well? Was he questioning his symptoms as too serious to ignore? Life could change in an instant. They had all just learned that in the most heartbreaking

If Things Were Different

way the night Mia died. Saylor imagined her children fatherless. She was too young to be a widow. She needed him. He would be okay. He had to be.

Saylor questioned if she should just drive straight to the hospital. But Penny suggested she come to the office, as the ambulance had not arrived yet. And she would call Saylor's cell phone back if she needed to. It immediately worried Saylor that Max had not been able to take her call. She didn't have time to waste, asking Penny questions, but she had wanted to know if Max could talk, if he was coherent. In a hurry, she left the kids with money for a pizza delivery, and then she ran out of the cottage, en route to her husband's office. Saylor had told her children to stay calm, and promised to update them as soon as she could. Brittany obviously could go home when she needed to, but Saylor ordered Sammy not to leave the cottage with Syd. She reassured them everything was going to be okay. And then Saylor prayed the entire drive there for that to be true.

*

The ambulance was parked in front of the building. Saylor saw it as soon as she drove too fast into the parking lot. She parked behind it. She didn't care if it was against the law or not, she was the wife of the co-owner of that business. She would take advantage of that luxury for the first time ever, if she were to be confronted about her emergency parking skills outside of the building. Saylor bolted through the front door, and ran through the empty lobby. Penny was not at the main desk.

She made her way down the wide corridor where more than a few employees were hovered near the door to Max's office. She pushed through the crowd, some had known who she was and stepped back for her to enter.

The first person she saw was Max. He was the only person she wanted to see. He was sitting upright on a gurney, and two paramedics were tending to him.

"Max!" Saylor blurted out, as she ran to him. "Are you okay?" Upright and conscious was obviously a plus in Saylor's mind already.

He nodded. "It could just be anxiety," he answered her, taking in a deeper breath than normal. "I have a pretty rapid heart rate and some trembling and serious sweating." She did notice his dark hair was matted above his eyebrows.

"He said his chest felt heavy," Penny chimed in. "That did it for me. I had to call 911."

Saylor glanced her way, and mouthed *thank you* to her as Max started to speak again. "I may have to go to the hospital for some tests, just precautionary heart checks."

"Absolutely," she told him, and it was unspoken but of course she was going along. Max knew that. He hated that he worried her, but the fact of the matter was he was extremely alarmed by how he felt too.

As the paramedics prepared Max to lie back on the gurney, it was Nash's turn to bolt through the door. The first person he saw was Saylor. She looked away from him as quickly as she had initially glanced at him.

"Max? What's happening?" Nash spoke, looking panicked for him.

"Probably anxiety," Max said, lifting his head off the gurney, "but I'm going to get my heart checked out just to be sure."

"Jesus," Nash stated. "You scared the hell out of me when I saw the ambulance and Saylor's jeep near it." He feared something had happened to Max, and it was confirmed by the not-so-subtle onlookers (their curious and concerned employees) outside of Max's office door.

"Yeah this might be a bit much, I could probably just have Saylor drive me to the hospital," Max was second guessing relying on the ambulance.

"That's ridiculous. Be smart about this. Go." Nash stated, and he looked at Saylor again but she had not turned in his direction. Not again since he came through the door. Like it or not, Nash was going to the hospital too. He wanted to be there for Max — and Saylor.

17

"So how do we know if your symptoms are anxiety or heart disease?" A male doctor with a full head of silver hair led into answering that question for both Max and Saylor in the examination room. "From what I've gathered so far, I'm concluding that your symptoms were anxiety-related. A few tests will confirm if anxiety caused your rapid heart rate, or if your rapid heart rate caused the anxiety." Max nodded, and Saylor spoke up.

"If it is anxiety," and Saylor hoped to God it was, "why didn't his medicine prevent the attack he had today?"

"During a full blown attack, medication will not give immediate relief of panic symptoms," the doctor explained. "Whatever bothers you is something you must work to cope with. Mind over matter is the magical cure." Saylor momentarily focused on what could be *bothering* her husband.

If Things Were Different

She stared at Max. She wondered what was on his mind, what had led to getting himself so seriously worked up that he thought he might be having a heart attack. He never spoke openly to her about his anxiety. It was as if he felt ashamed or embarrassed by it. It was something that Saylor didn't understand and could not relate to, but beginning now she promised herself to be more in tune to Max's issue. She would never again assume just because he popped a pill, he was consequently better. Today's scare had taught her that.

The doctor told Max that he ordered both a stress test and an electrocardiogram for him. When Saylor and Max were left alone, to wait for a nurse to escort Max to his tests, he was quiet.

"How do you feel now?" Saylor asked him.

"I'm okay. I'm glad I'm having the tests done as a precaution, but it sounds like it was just my nerves in overdrive."

"Is work stressing you out that much?" Saylor asked, unaware of any problems within the company but not oblivious to the fact that things can change daily with any business.

Before Max could answer her, they were interrupted by a nurse who needed to whisk him away. Saylor was asked to move to a waiting room down the hall. She walked with them until the nurse pointed her in the direction of where she could have a seat and wait. For now, that waiting area was empty.

But not for long. Just long enough for her to send a reassuring text to Sammy. And then Nash made his way in there. Saylor really wasn't all that surprised he was there.

"How did you know I was in here?" Saylor asked, feeling like now was not the time for this. For him. For them to be alone again.

"I asked at the main desk." Nash sat down in the chair right next to hers. Their shoulders touched briefly, until Saylor subtly moved in her seat. "So what did the doctor say? And what's going on now?"

"He thinks it's anxiety, like Max had some sort of attack that gave him heart palpitations and the other symptoms. He is having a stress test and an EKG done to be sure his heart checks out as normal."

"That's all good then," Nash stated, feeling some relief himself.

"Yes, let's hope," Saylor replied, fidgeting in her chair, crossing one leg over the other, and then switching which leg she had crossed over the other.

"Has he been taking Prozac still?" Nash's question caught Saylor a bit off guard. That was personal information. Maybe she shouldn't have been surprised though. The two of them were together as much as a married couple. And they were close.

"He said he has been," Saylor responded. "Is everything going well at M&N? Is there something stressing him out there that he's purposely keeping from me? I was about to ask him that question when the nurse interrupted us a little while ago." Saylor's first thought was financial trouble, but that idea came out of nowhere because she had no reason to believe it.

If Things Were Different

"If you're asking about financial woes, no, we are far from trouble. We're sailing." Saylor smiled at his word choice. Her father used to say that in reference to many things. "And being busy never seems to stress out Max any more than the rest of us."

"Well I have to get him to talk to me later. I'm just really worried about him," Saylor added. As she should be. An ambulance was called. And they were in the hospital now.

"He'll be fine," Nash attempted to calm her. He felt a little unnerved though at the idea of the two of them having a chance *to talk later, to be alone together later*. He chided himself for his own ridiculous thoughts. They were married. They had shared fifteen years of that togetherness. Things were different now though. Nash knew it. And so did Saylor.

"You don't have to wait with me," Saylor stated, partially hoping he would leave her there alone.

"It's not like I have anywhere else to be, or anyone to go home to."

"Have you heard from Londyn since she left? Did her flight land in LA?"

"No, and I don't expect her to check in. That's not what almost unmarried people do, is it?"

"I wouldn't know," she told him, and then she lowered her voice even though they were the only two people in the waiting area. "And I'm not going to ever know either. Max needs me. He's my husband. For life."

Nash nodded his head. He instantly picked up on how she never said she needed Max. Just that he needed her. "You're forgetting, or trying to ignore how you really feel. That will catch up to you one day. I think it already has."

"I'm not talking about this with you. Not here." *And not ever again*, she wanted to add, but recognized how unrealistic that would seem.

They both sat there in silence for awhile, knowing the other was thinking the same thing.

A few hours earlier in the day, when Londyn left the condo — and left Nash — Saylor knew she needed to escape there. Being alone with him was happening more frequently than it ever had, and she didn't trust herself. Nash's life had changed practically overnight. First, Mia's tragic death. And then Londyn wanted out. Never in her life had Saylor ever thought she would root for the two of them to stay together. She needed them to be married. That was the roadblock for Nash and Saylor, and it had been for many years. It was tempting and risky for them without that boundary.

Saylor had been in his arms when the condo lost power. She had been crying over Londyn's decision to leave Nash, leaving him free — and her feeling torn. In the complete darkness, she immediately pulled out of his embrace.

"The wind must have knocked out the power," Nash stated. "I'll grab a flashlight and some candles." He stepped back, knowing exactly where he was even in the pitch dark. That was his home, he could walk through it blindfolded. And right now the complete darkness was the equivalent.

If Things Were Different

"Wait, I can't see anything in front of me," Saylor spoke, holding up her hand in front of her face and she was barely able to see the outline of it. "Just walk me over to the front door, and I'll go. I should leave now."

Nash took her hand in the air between them. "You should probably wait out the remainder of the storm. Driving isn't the smartest idea right now. There could be power lines down."

Staying wasn't the smartest idea right now either, Saylor knew that for certain. He was still holding her hand. "Nash, I really have to go. I can't be here, alone, with you like this." Her honesty pushed him further.

"Don't over think it," Nash said, because he knew her so well. Everything was processed in her mind, and over thought most of the time. "Just feel it." His lips met hers before she had the chance to process anything. What was happening just happened. She kissed him back. With force. With passion. This wasn't the dock on the waterfront where other people were present. This wasn't the beach in the middle of the night that was in close proximity to the cottage. This was a private place where the two of them were alone. Behind closed doors. Inside four walls that protected them from judgment. If what they were doing were to ever be found out, lives would change. But in his arms, Saylor was caught up in how nothing had changed. She still knew every inch of his body. And he remembered well how to satisfy her while he drove her to the brink of insanity. They kissed. They touched. Their clothes were stripped hurriedly and fell to the hardwood floor along with them. Their naked bodies were entangled in a passion that had never died.

For those moments, Saylor didn't have a husband. She never thought of Max or her children. She found herself all in with Nash again. She was young and free and high on only him. She was in love with him. She craved and succumbed to the way he made her feel when he touched her. And when it was over, reality and panic and fear all set in hard and fast. Saylor rushed to dress, to flee that condo, and to abandon Nash and the memory of what they had done together.

Still seated side by side in the waiting area, Saylor felt sickened at the thought of what she did. Nash had nothing to lose. His family was already gone. But she had absolutely everything to fight for, and to keep close, as hers. The greatest battle ahead of her though was going to be the blazing feelings inside of her that were resurrected for a man she should have left in her past.

18

Their kids were both on the sofa when Saylor and Max came home from the hospital. She had first driven him to the parking lot of M&N to retrieve his vehicle. And then she followed him back to the cottage. She was going to keep a close eye on Max like that for awhile. The doctor confirmed his attack today had stemmed from anxiety, as both of the tests depicted his heart as healthy.

"Daddy!" Syd ran to him and he immediately picked her up and squeezed her. "Is your heart okay?" Max smiled. She had his heart for sure.

"It's just fine, honey."

"Did the doctor give you a band-aid?"

"Nope, no band-aid. He just made sure my heart is beating okay, and it is, so I came home. We can all get back to normal now," Max told everyone. Saylor knew he was uncomfortable with being hovered over. She made eye contact with Sammy then, and he knew better. He would ask her any questions later that he had.

"We stayed inside, like you told us to," Sammy said to Saylor, "but the guys and Brittany are hanging out on the beach tonight…"

"Go on," Saylor told him, "and thank you for your help with Syd."

Sammy smiled at her, and then looked back at Max before he walked out the front door. "I'm glad you're okay, dad."

"Me too, buddy. Thanks."

Once Sammy left, Saylor told Syd it was time for a bubble bath. After a squeal, Saylor followed those little legs down the hallway to fill the clawfoot bathtub. Once she had her settled with a just-right water temperature and a few bath toys, Saylor left the bathroom door open and walked out into the living room for a moment to check on Max, who was lying down on the sofa.

"Before you ask, I'm good," he said to her in a snarky tone. She assumed he was cranky because of the commotion surrounding him today. Things like that easily embarrassed him.

Saylor nodded. "Are we going to talk about why you felt the way you did at the office today? Did something happen to make you upset or nervous?"

Max eyed her from the sofa. "You really shouldn't leave her unattended in the bathtub. We don't need another crisis."

If Things Were Different

She immediately was miffed. Saylor was more than capable of taking care of their daughter. She trusted Syd in the bathtub, and sometimes left her alone to play or soak for a several minutes. "This isn't something that you can just ignore. We are going to talk about it. Man up, Max. Communication isn't that damn difficult!" And then she stormed back down the hallway and slammed the bathroom door. She would just tell Syd that it slipped out of her grip.

✱

Max was in their bed after Saylor read Syd a storybook and then tucked her into her own bed across the hall. Saylor was still wearing the same clothes she had on all day, cut-offs and a tank top. She slipped out of both, and stood in their bedroom in her panties and bra. Before she stepped into their master bathroom to shower, she looked at Max, lying on his back on his side of their bed.

He knew she was angry, but dammit so was he. Max was both angry and scared. Scared of losing Saylor, and he didn't quite know how to tell her that. She wanted communication from him about this, so he at least had to try. But he assumed Saylor already knew of what he was going to tell her.

"Why are we mad at each other?" Max asked her, stopping her from entering the bathroom. She stood there in her delicates and Max looked at her no differently than if she was standing there in a nun's habit. They were comfortable in their marriage, and at ease around each other. But the excitement, if there ever was any, was fleeting. "I was sent home from the ER tonight with good news. We should be happy."

"Yes, you were," Saylor responded only to the second half of what he stated. "and you're right."

"I don't like to talk about how I feel when I can't control being nervous or anxious," he admitted, and Saylor remained still where she stood. Finally, he was honestly speaking to her about this. "You said for me to man up. Well nothing makes me feel less masculine than when I'm upset and unable to focus on anything but my trembling hands and shortness of breath."

"Max," Saylor responded, "that's not what I meant. I need you to talk to me. I have so many thoughts racing through my mind. At one point today I wondered if we were in financial trouble at M&N." She didn't add that Nash reassured her otherwise.

"The business is fine. Flourishing," he added. "It's me and how I feel about the same thing that started to cause me this damn anxiety years back," he paused. "Londyn called me today." Saylor's eyes widened, and she stayed quiet. "She was at the airport, headed for a fresh beginning, a new life, but I'm sure you already knew that." Max was referring to the time she spent with Nash in the hospital waiting room. He wasn't too pleased to see them together once his tests were completed and he looked for his wife to leave.

Saylor wondered if contacting Max was Londyn's last jab at her. *Here, you can have Nash but not before I taint your image in the eyes of your own husband.* "She asked me to come to the condo today. She was all packed, and ready to flee the only life she's known as an adult. Nash was there, too." Saylor believed she may as well admit that. She couldn't, and wouldn't, reveal everything to him though. Right now she was trying her damndest to block her memory of her moment of temporary insanity.

"Just like that, their marriage is over, huh?" Max asked, sounding as if he was mocking them both for giving up on their commitment.

"I don't think it was instantaneous," Saylor spoke up. "They lost Mia. They're both in a tremendous amount of pain. And the fact is, Max, they don't know how to turn to each other. I'm not sure they've ever been capable of that."

"Well I'm happy for Londyn, because I think she needs something for herself now more than ever, and I told her that," Max said, pulling his knees up to his bare chest underneath the navy blue sheet on the bed. "But I think Nash is an insensitive jerk to let her go, especially at a time like this. She was the mother of his only child, for God's sake!"

Saylor caught on quickly that Max's anger toward Nash was what set off the alarm to his body's extreme anxiety today. She too secretly panicked, right now, knowing what she did and how her husband would never be able to cope with that. Not ever. He was a straight-arrow, a do-gooder. He would in no way understand her mistake, her moment of selfishness when she hadn't a care in the world.

"I wish they would stay together, too," Saylor finally spoke, "but that's obviously not for us to decide, or judge. Max, are you insinuating that Londyn's news over the phone today was what upset you to the point of the panic attack?" Saylor hoped with all of her being that Londyn had not talked too openly with Max as she had with her and Nash. She wanted to right a wrong, she had pretty much summed that up to them. Londyn was stepping out of the way for her and Nash to be together again. Saylor loathed the thought of Londyn being right. They had no self control when they were in each other's orbit. They did belong together. They had a powerful, passionate attraction. It was all true because she and Nash had turned to each other the moment Londyn left.

"It's not what she said. It's where I allowed my mind to go once she ended our call," Max admitted. "Nash is a confident man. I've grown up alongside of him. I recruited him to partner in business with me because he's got what it takes to get things done, to get what he wants. If he wants a sale, he gets a fucking sale." Saylor wanted to stop him, to tell him to calm down, but Max was finally opening up to her, so she allowed him to go on. "He has nothing left at home. No family anymore. No wife. No daughter. Only self-centered Nash. I think we both know what he's going to want now. I can't take it, Saylor. I can't stand the thought of him stealing you away from me. I'll kill him first."

"Stop it!" Saylor spoke adamantly. She was trembling inside, and it did not help that she was standing there nearly naked. She forced herself not to think about how just hours earlier Nash had taken off that very bra and panties. His hands were on her, his body meshed with hers. Saylor knew that if Max knew, he would never forgive her. He couldn't kill anyone though. But *he* would die inside. What she did would kill him. "Have a little faith in us, in our marriage." Saying those words instantly left Saylor feeling like the adulterer she was. She could hardly get the words out without swallowing hard to push down the lump of guilt in her throat.

"It's not that I don't trust you," Max told her, and that was beyond difficult for Saylor to hear right now. "It's him. And I don't know how to stand on my own two feet and tell Nash that without shaking like a leaf. I cannot control this anxiety that he's caused. I want to man up and remind him in no uncertain terms that you are *my* wife, because I know that he has the power to change that one day." Saylor could see the tears in his eyes from where she stood halfway across the room. In their lifelong friendship, Max was the one with the greater need. He had needed Nash to fend off the bullies, to fit in with the popular crowd, to be his voice when he didn't have the courage, to help him spearhead a successful business, and lastly — to unwillingly give up a woman, and inevitably allow Max to have her.

"Max…" she spoke, feeling sickened by this. By his pain. And especially by her actions with Nash. "You need to put that out of your head, or you are going to drive yourself crazy."

"Can you tell me that none of what I am saying is true? Can you promise me that if he wants you, you will turn him away, and choose me again?"

"I already made my choice," Saylor spoke vaguely. She was referring to fifteen years ago when she married him, not right now. She walked over to their bed and sat down beside him. He bent forward and she cradled his head on her lap, running her fingers through his black, wavy hair. Max may have looked strong on the exterior, but Saylor had been the only one to witness his greatest weakness tearing him down to shreds.

19

Saylor sat outside on the front porch just hours after Max made his emergency trip to the hospital, and when he had broken down about his fear of Nash taking her away from him. It was plain and simple. Without Londyn, Nash was a free man. He wanted to be a free man. And he would also want Saylor back. It was only a matter of time. Max had always lived with that fear, tucked into a vacant corner of his mind. Saylor's guilt now overwhelmed her. She couldn't change what she *just did* with Nash. But she could stop it from ever happening again.

The night air was more humid than usual, and Saylor thought about going back inside to bed. She doubted she would be able to sleep though. The moment she planted her bare feet on the floorboards, her cell phone buzzed. *It was the middle of the night. And it was Nash.*

If Things Were Different

Are you awake? He asked.

Yes. She responded. And that's what instantly unnerved Saylor about herself. If she was going to recommit to Max, why had she already taken a step backward? There was such a thing as ignoring a message. No reply meant not interested.

We need to talk. Nash began.

We temporarily lost our minds. It can't happen again. Saylor warned him. And she had to delete these messages from her phone, in fear of someone else coming across them, reading them, and knowing she was a cheat.

Max deserves to know the truth. I don't want to hurt him anymore than you do, believe me. But he has to know. Nash was adamant.

Absolutely not! You know him as well as I do. It will destroy him. Saylor's mind flashed back to earlier this evening when her husband fell apart in her arms, on their bed. That was something she would never be able to explain to Nash. Max was a man who needed people as crutches. Nash could hold and carry his own. And Saylor had realized over time that she also became someone Max counted on to lift him up, to make him feel whole. He couldn't stand on his own two feet without someone by his side. He needed someone to balance him. Nash was that person for him in his business life. And Saylor, as his wife, was the beacon in his personal life. Max wasn't a weak man. He just lacked the confidence to stand alone.

He's stronger than you are giving him credit for. Nash defended his best friend.

Saylor agreed, but she also was the woman Max let his guard down with. Guys were different together, one was always trying to outdo and out-tough the other.

I'm staying with him. I have a family to hold together. Saylor eventually replied back, and that was the final text exchanged between the two of them in the middle of the night.

✼

The following day, Max returned to work. Saylor had suggested he come home for lunch, or meet her and the kids somewhere fun. He told her another day would be better, because he likely had too much missed work to catch up on. Saylor never responded to his excuse. She had only thought to herself how he was *all work and no play*.

Syd was building a sandcastle on the beach, and Saylor had been watching her from a far. She promised her if she kept busy, playing solo all morning while she worked on one grant project, the two of them would have a picnic lunch at the park. That was going to be their *something fun* for the day.

They chose Jersey Mike's sub sandwiches to eat at the park under a shade tree. Syd's mop of blonde curls was matted to her forehead and around her full face with rosy cheeks. "You need to cool off, you've been outside much of the day," Saylor smiled at her, as she watched her take too big of a bite of her sandwich and attempted to chew it all.

"I like it outside," Syd spoke after she had chewed most of the food in her mouth.

"Me too," Saylor wholeheartedly agreed with her.

"It's a happy day," Syd stated as a matter of fact.

"It is? Why do you think today is happier than any other day?" Saylor quizzed her.

"Because you are happy, mommy. I feel happy when you are happy." Syd took another bite, and Saylor set her sandwich down on her lap, on the paper it was wrapped in prior.

"Well being with you makes me happy," Saylor took a napkin and dabbed the mayonnaise off Syd's chin.

"Does being with Sammy make you happy, too?" Syd asked, and this time she had too much food in her mouth. Saylor reminded her to be polite and chew and swallow before she spoke. And to take a drink of her lemonade from the straw cup on the ground beside her.

Saylor nodded. "Absolutely."

"And Daddy?" Saylor expected Max to be next in line in this series of questions, but what she had not anticipated was how she felt about answering that question. *When was the last time she saw Max truly happy? Smiling? Joking? Laughing? Having a drink with her, or walking hand-in-hand along the beach with her?*

"Of course, Daddy too," Saylor replied, her voice trailing off.

"And Nash?" Syd piped up, proudly having thought of another person in their circle, and Saylor creased her brow.

"Nash works with daddy. He's his best friend. He's sort of like an uncle to you and Sammy. And he was Mia's daddy." Saylor somehow thought it was necessary to recite everything Nash was in connection to all of the them — except for herself.

"I know all of that," Syd stated. "So, is Nash happy, mommy?"

"He's missing Mia so much, sweetie. It's going to take time for him to find his smile again." That was the best way Saylor could answer the question — without admitting that Nash does make her happy.

Syd finished eating her sandwich, but Saylor had hardly touched hers. She wanted to play at the park, and Saylor told her to go over to the playground and she would soon follow once she threw away their lunch trash.

Syd ran ahead and Saylor watched her from afar. She immediately befriended a little boy on the slide, and Saylor noticed someone, who clearly looked like a grandmother, seated on a nearby bench watching both of them. Saylor walked over there, and at first she stood near the bench that the silver-haired plump woman was seated on.

"She's mine," Saylor immediately spoke, in reference to Syd, as she walked up.

The older woman chuckled. "I saw the two of you having lunch under that shade tree. It's a good day to enjoy the park. I told my grandson that I will sit here and watch him play all day long. That's about all these old bones can do anymore. No swinging or sliding for me." She laughed out loud again, and Saylor did too. "Sit, join me. The littles seem to be having a good time together." Saylor sat down, leaving enough space between them to fit another person.

"I'm Saylor, my daughter's name is Syd."

"I thought so. You're a Bach," the older woman spoke with confidence. "My son-in-law works for that solar company you and your husband own. I'm Mollie, and my grandson is Jax."

"Oh that's wonderful. How long has your son-in-law worked for my husband?" Saylor wanted to stress that Max was in charge, not her, so she did not come across as insensitive or too uppity to know her own employees by name and face.

"Under five years, maybe three and half or four," she stated. "Good pay, good benefits. He married my youngest daughter, and Jax is their son." Saylor glanced again at the little boy, with wildly spiked hair, who was playing with Syd on the slide.

"I'm married to Max, one of the owners of M&N," Saylor offered.

"You and your family live on the beach, right?" she asked, and Saylor thought of the roughly ten thousand people who lived in Morehead City, and how some people could still manage to know details about everyone else's lives. Maybe the spotlight on them came with owning a successful, profitable business.

"Yes, we do."

"And the Parker fellow, the other owner, he just lost his daughter. How tragic. My son-in-law attended the funeral. He said it was the saddest darn thing he'd ever seen."

"I agree." Saylor really didn't know what else to say. She was somewhat uncomfortable with the prying. She knew this woman was just making conversation, but this was other people's private business that had nothing to do with her. Despite the son-in-law as an employee connection.

"And now I just heard at my bridge club yesterday that the Parker guy's wife left him. She's a model and apparently she took off permanently for Los Angeles. That might be too much change too fast and so soon after such loss."

Saylor kept her eyes on Syd, and she really wanted to do was call her away from her new little friend on the slide and tell her they had to go home. But she looked as if she was having fun, so Saylor would just tolerate nosy Mollie's chatter.

And the gossip continued.

"I lived next door to Sarah Parker," she stated, and if Saylor had been sipping on the lemonade she had with her lunch, she would have choked and spit it out right about now. She hadn't heard Sarah Parker's name in a very long time. She was Nash's mother, who died eight years ago.

"She was a nice lady," Saylor offered, hoping Mollie had not been well informed of Nash's past when he was dating her and ended up marrying another young woman he had gotten pregnant. But something told Saylor that she knew that story, too.

"And she thought the world of you, Saylor. She was heartbroken for her son when he had to let you go. That model was a beautiful girl and she and the Parker boy raised their baby girl together like what was expected of them, but as it turns out, they weren't happy."

"I suppose we all do what we have to do sometimes," Saylor responded the only way she knew how, other than being rude.

"Yes we do," Mollie spoke up, "but let me tell you something… when you get to be my age, you look back and you wonder what in the hell you were thinking at times. Who cares what's morally right, or expected of you! It's your life. Live it happily, or one day those regrets will become so haunting you won't be able to sleep at night." Between Syd's questions during lunch, and now Mollie, the topic of being *happy* was getting some mileage today.

Saylor let those words sink in. Mollie's prying may have granted her the knowledge about the many people in Morehead City, but she had absolutely no idea how torn Saylor felt at this stage in her life. *She was happy with Max and their children. They were a family. But, if she had been entirely happy with her life, why had she given in to her old desires for Nash? And why was she still contemplating all of the what ifs she could still have with him in this life?*

"It's important to be happy. That's good advice," Saylor reiterated, as she stood up from the park bench they shared. She suddenly had somewhere she needed to be.

20

Saylor held Syd's hand as they walked through the entrance of M&N Solar Energy Development. Penny immediately reacted to seeing Syd. This was hardly a regular occurrence for Saylor to be there so often, and it was especially out of the ordinary for either of Max's children to be on the premises.

"Hello there," Penny spoke, before she reached for something in the bottom drawer of a file cabinet. "It's good to see you, Miss Sydney." Syd smiled, as she was rarely called by her entire first name. "What can I do for you two?"

If Things Were Different

"We're hoping Max isn't too busy to see us," Saylor replied.

"He's not held up in a meeting right now, so I can let him know you are here," Penny offered. "And if you want, I have some coloring pages for a sweet little girl. You can take them with you to your daddy's office, or keep me company out here. I'm really good at coloring." Penny winked, and showed Syd what she already had in her hand.

"Can I color out here in the lobby with Penny, mommy?" Syd was taken with that environment — the high ceiling, the windowed walls. And the special attention.

"Sure. I'll have daddy come out here to say hi after I talk to him for a few minutes. Thanks Penny," Saylor added, as she walked alone down the long corridor. She didn't need to be announced. It might be fun to surprise her husband.

She knocked twice, turned the door handle, and peeked her head through the doorway. Max was seated at his desk, punching keys on his computer. He looked up. His glasses were low on his nose. "Saylor, what's going on?" He pushed back his chair and looked as if he was going to stand up, but he didn't.

"Just a visit," she smiled as she made her way into his office. "Syd's in the lobby, coloring with Penny. She's really sweet with her."

Max creased his brow, either in annoyance or confusion. He wasn't even sure which at this point. "A visit? I'm working. I have a company to run."

"I'm aware of that, but maybe I just wanted to stop in here and make sure you're feeling alright?" That wasn't entirely the reason.

"I'm fine. I'm good. You could have called or sent a text for that."

Saylor shrugged. "We had a picnic lunch at the park, so we were close by." She then sat down in one of the two chairs facing his desk. Max rolled his chair forward then, took off his reading glasses, and placed both of his elbows on the desktop. "There's another reason I'm here, Max." She definitely had her husband's attention. "I want you to take a break. Let's have some fun for a few days." She wanted to say, *all you do is work. It's summer time. Let's throw some impromptu times in the mix, and make some memories with the kids. Change things up a bit. Let's choose happiness*. Silver-haired Mollie's words from the park bench were ringing in her ears. And Saylor's guilt was eating away at her conscious. She had chosen Nash in the moment — temporarily and insanely. But now, she needed to choose Max and their life together. And she wanted him to help her do just that.

"Saylor, our kids love water. We live on the beach. Where else could we possibly go? People choose vacation spots exactly like our cottage to be that close to the sand and the ocean. I'll bet if you ask our kids, they wouldn't even want to go anywhere else right now. Sammy is hung up on his friends at the beach this summer, and Syd is happy wherever we are."

Okay, so this wasn't so much about the kids. It was Saylor and her need to get away with Max. She wanted to pull him from work, and the two of them away from any distractions. *Nash.* She wanted Max's attention to be on her, and hers on him. If he had been so frantic to lose her, he hadn't done anything to hold on tighter to her. Their life, their family, was enough for Max. Saylor wanted it to be *enough* for her, too. But right now it wasn't. She even questioned if a getaway was the answer. But she was desperate to try.

A double knock of hard knuckles interrupted them as the closed office door swung open. Nash's long legs in khaki pants stepped through the doorway. "Oh, hey… I'm interrupting —"

"No, you're fine," Max waved him in, as he saw how Saylor reacted to his presence. She smiled as she made eye contact with him, then she looked down at her lap. And Nash's entire face lit up like the 4th of July fireworks. That was nothing new. Max had seen it for years. He was sure Londyn had as well. That's why it was finally easy for her to walk away. In the midst of her terrible grief, she had surrendered. Max wasn't going to be like Londyn. He wouldn't give up what was his.

"You sure are stopping by here a lot lately." Nash's comment was true. "Checking up on the old ball and chain?"

Saylor forced a laugh. "You could say that. Maybe you could help me convince him to take a break from here for a few days? You could run the show solo, right?" Nash didn't like where this was going. Saylor seemed desperate to reclaim her life with Max. And right in front of him no less. Nash cringed inside.

"Absolutely. Are you still not feeling well?" he directed his question and his eyes on Max.

"I'm good," Max shook his head, as if to brush off the attention on his health again. "My wife just thinks we need a vacation."

Saylor refrained from looking Nash's way. But Nash forced her to when he spoke. "No one leaves the beach in the summer!"

"That's what I just said!" Max blurted out, and all but high-fived Nash. Saylor could have glared back at him, at both of them.

"Forget I mentioned it," Saylor sounded defeated.

"Nah, I'm just teasing," Nash spoke, and Max noticed the concern for Saylor on his face. "You could go on a cruise or something? We used to enjoy those." He spoke of his family as if it was in the past, and sadly it was. And then Max saw the look of empathy that passed over Saylor's eyes.

"Wasn't Mia's first cruise a Disney one?" she asked him.

Nash smiled. "Yeah, Londyn and I were actually just talking about that last week. She loved to travel with us, and that's probably because we started her out really young." Nash felt that sick feeling bubbling up from his stomach to his chest. There would never be another site to see, or place to travel to, for his Mia.

"Mia was lucky in that regard," Max stated, but he felt sad speaking of her in the past tense. *Gone, but not forgotten.* "We really haven't traveled that much with our kids."

If Things Were Different

Saylor wanted to say, *see, we should!* But she didn't.

"Well then do it — before it's too late," Nash added. "There's always the Smoky Mountains for a few days of cabin time?" Nash and Max were both fisherman, and had taken many trips like that together over the years.

Max overlooked the fact that Nash had mentioned a place that harbored good times for them. He only focused on Nash's words, *before it's too late.*

Had Nash only made reference to himself for the sudden and tragic way that his family dissolved? Or, was he thinking right here and now? Before it's too late for you and your wife. Before she's mine again. Max inhaled a deep breath, slowly through his nostrils. Mind over matter, he thought to himself. He wouldn't allow Nash to win.

"I may be giving you a few days to hold down the fort, once we decide where we are going," Max spoke directly to Nash. "I guess first we'll see if the kids want to go with us?" Max now looked at Saylor. "We could make it a second honeymoon... we have hit the fifteenth year mark." Saylor knew what Max was doing now. He was purposely marking his territory, his wife, in front of Nash. Earlier, he had no interest in taking her anywhere. This whole idea had gone haywire. And all Saylor wanted to do now was leave. But Max wasn't through. It was as if he had finally grown a pair of balls with Nash, and in front of her. Maybe it was because she was there. Saylor fueled both of them to act as if they had a claim to her. And right now, she was fed up.

"Any suggestions there, Nash? I'm sure you're the man when it comes to romantic getaways?" Max added.

"What the hell is that supposed to mean?" Nash was instantly offended. "Don't insinuate that I wasn't faithful to Londyn." He had been, Saylor assumed, by his reaction. Up until a day ago, they both had been true to their spouses. It was Saylor's turn to cringe. Some of Max's anxiety was rubbing off on her. Her hands were clammy and all she wanted to do was bolt out of there, and into the lobby to snatch Syd so they could both get out of there. She assumed Syd was the only one of them enjoying herself there today. Her presence had obviously gotten these two men riled up.

Max held up both of his hands. "Just asking your opinion, because you travel more than I do."

"Take your wife wherever she wants to go. That's my advice," Nash said. "Because if she's happy, if she's wearing a smile on her face and you can see fire in her eyes, that's all that matters." Saylor blushed, and Nash turned on his heels and walked out of that office. Whatever he came in there for could wait. He said what he meant. He felt cocky and confident as he left. He was the only man who could put that fire in Saylor's eyes. Max had his chance. And after those fifteen years that he boasted about, he still hadn't made it happen.

Nash took his phone out of the pocket of his khakis as he walked the long corridor toward the lobby. He sent Saylor a brief text.

Let me be the one to whisk you away.

21

Saylor stood up when Nash walked out. "I should go. We can talk about this later. Like you said, we'll see where the kids might want to go." What Saylor wanted to say was *just forget it*.

Max stood after she did. "Do I make you happy, Saylor?"

"What kind of question is that? You and the kids are my life." Nash had planted that doubtful seed in Max's mind again, and Saylor worried about his anxiety overwhelming him.

Max walked around his desk and met his wife in front of it. She reached for him first, and he pulled her close. "I know he thinks he can make you happier."

Saylor pulled out of his embrace, and forced her eyes on him. "You need to stop this."

He kissed her on the forehead, but stayed silent.

"Walk with me out into the lobby. I promised Syd she could see you."

In the lobby, they found Syd on Nash's shoulders. He was like a kid again, bouncing her around until she couldn't stop the giggles. Penny had obviously gotten a kick out of seeing one of her bosses in fun mode. It's not as if that had been the first time though. Nash was known to be the entertaining one in that building.

"Daddy!" Syd exclaimed from atop of Nash's shoulders. And Nash turned to both Saylor and Max. He reached up his arms and lifted her down to the floor, where on her feet she ran to Max. He swooped her up the moment she was close enough and he kissed her chubby cheeks, two times on each side. And she giggled again. "I like it here with Penny and Nash!" Max smiled.

"I'm glad you're having fun, baby girl." He held onto her when Syd asked him to take a look at the picture she colored with Penny. As they made their way over to Penny's desk, Saylor stood alone with Nash.

"You okay?" she asked him, because she knew. She could read him so well still.

"Uh, not really. I used to have a baby girl of my own."

"The way you were with Syd right now brought some of those times back, I'm sure. You were so good with Mia. She was such a daddy's girl."

"Stop, unless you want to see a grown man cry in the lobby of his own business," Nash stated, in an attempt to be funny. It was easier to be funny than sad.

"I'm sorry," she told him.

"Me too. It sucks." They both turned their heads to Max and Syd who were laughing with Penny.

"Do you have your phone on you?" Nash asked her spontaneously. He needed her in his life now more than ever.

"No, it's in the jeep. Why?"

"You'll see soon enough."

Saylor creased her brow at him just as Max and Syd were coming their way.

✱

At dinner, Max was the first one to bring up a possible family vacation.

"A vacation? Seriously dad? We live on the beach," Sammy had said, and Saylor thought — like father, like son. Max chuckled as he glanced across the table at Saylor, and she rolled her eyes. "Count me out, unless we can take Brittany along."

"You're pushing it, Sam," Saylor spoke up. "You're fifteen, you are not doing anything overnight with a girl." Sammy shrugged as if he tried.

"I don't want to go with you guys," Sammy spoke up again. "I could stay at the cottage myself, and the three of you could get away somewhere."

"Seriously?" Saylor chimed in again. "Do you really think we are that naive?" Again, her boy with raging hormones clearly only had his first serious girlfriend on his mind.

"You could always stay behind with Syd, you know, watch her for us while your mom and I get away…" Max laughed out loud at Sammy's defiant facial expression, and Saylor shook her head no.

"This obviously was a bad idea all around," Saylor stated. "Let's just continue as is, on this beach, working our butts off, and not doing anything too out of the ordinary." That implication was for Max, and only Max. She knew how to step outside of the box and enjoy herself. Saylor's mind flashed to Nash. She immediately forced the image of them two of them having sex on the floor out of her head.

If Things Were Different

Sammy asked to be excused, and Syd left the table with him. That left Max and Saylor alone. "You're mad," he said first.

"No, just disappointed," she spoke honestly.

"Travel just doesn't fit with who we are as a family right now. We have a teenager who really doesn't want to be seen with us," Max laughed.

"You're right about that," she told him. "It also may be time for you to have a man-to-man talk with your son. He seems like he's getting really serious about Brittany."

Max nodded. "I'll get on that." Saylor thanked him with her eyes and her smile. She started to stand up from the table, to clear the dinner plates. "We can't always get what we want. We're responsible adults, working hard, and raising kids. It's our stage of life. Fun is for the youth." Sometimes, the things that Max said could completely unnerve her. It was as if he was taking a jab at her. He believed he knew life better than she did. And she should just suck it up and deal.

"So you're telling me to grow up?" she asked him, standing in front of her chair, and glaring down at him, still seated across the table. He shrugged. No words, just a childish shrug. *And he was the adult in this relationship?* "I mean, really, Max? Fun is not *just* for the youth! If you cannot live a little, and enjoy life, then you're missing out. The days and nights are running together, the years will be gone before we know it." She wanted to ask if he'd ever heard what the ocean sounded like in the dark of night when everything else around was still? Had he ever drank a beer in the middle of the day just to seek the buzz and push everything else out of his mind? Had he ever made love on the hardwood floor in the aftermath of a storm? Yes, she was thinking of Nash and all he could give her. She needed more than what her husband could offer. She tried. But there was going to be no changing him. And she was tired of trying.

"Sounds to me like you're going through a mid-life crisis or something. What's changed with you?" Max asked her.

"I am pushing forty years old," she partially agreed with him, "and I guess I just want to make sure life doesn't pass me by." *Without regrets.*

"You've always been a little wilder than me," Max chuckled, as he was the last one to stand up from the table. "I hope Syd doesn't take after you in that regard." Whether Max was teasing or not, Saylor was offended. She certainly did hope that her little girl would grow up with a fire in her soul. And she especially wanted for her to never allow anyone else to smother that inferno. Because that was exactly how she felt in her marriage. Especially right now.

"Well if you think I need to get this ache to travel out of my system, I will have an opportunity to do so for work," Saylor began. And she began with a lie.

"With work?" She had Max's attention in their kitchen as they both stood near the sink, with dirty dishes in their hands.

"Yes, I'm writing a grant for a library in Charlotte and I'll need to go there for a few days." The City of Charlotte was a five-hour drive from Morehead City.

"On site? Since when?" Max asked.

If Things Were Different

"Since I was invited. Believe it or not, I've had requests like this before but I've just never taken anyone up on it. I want to go and get a better feel for the program that I'm fighting for. And again, it'll be my chance to get the travel bug out of my system."

"Okay, if you think you have to do this," Max stated, nonchalantly. He didn't even ask why she hadn't mentioned the trip before now. It seemed like a fair plan to him though. He didn't have to disrupt his work, or travel anywhere. And, hopefully, the travel and time away would appease Saylor.

"Sammy can help some with Syd, but I'll sign her up for day camps to free him up."

"Whatever you need to do," Max told her, and Saylor felt an instant pang of guilt. Yes, she needed to do this. And, right or wrong, she was going to do this.

"Okay then, I'll accept the invitation to go."

22

Saylor waited until her family was asleep. From the pale yellow rocker, she sent a text to Nash in the middle of the night. There was a chance he would not even see her message until morning. But she had waited long enough. Max had let her down. Her need to flee outweighed her guilt right now.

Whisk me away. Do it before I change my mind.

He was awake, and Saylor's message had jolted him far from any sleepy state he had been in prior.

Absolutely I will! Nash responded.

Just a few days. I have "grant work." Saylor emphasized.

Leave it all to me. At this point, Nash didn't care where they went together. He only wanted to be with her. But he would plan the most special getaway for Saylor because she deserved one.

Thank you. I need this. Saylor replied.

You're welcome. I need you. She read his words twice, and then deleted their exchange of messages.

If Things Were Different

Saylor harbored both excitement and apprehension. She was an adult. A parent. A mother. A wife. She had lived four decades. She was supposed to do what was expected of her, and to be responsible. And then there was the part of her who just didn't care anymore. Or, who cared enough to fan the fire that had reignited in her soul.

*

Two days later, Saylor had prepared her family to function without her for a few days. Max nodded along when she told him not to work late, to reheat the meals she had prepared, or to choose take-out. She gave him a list of the day camps Syd was signed up for, with the drop-off and pick-up times. Sammy was less compliant when she told him what he had to do. He was allowed to hang out with his friends on the beach during the day when Syd was not there, and at night after Max was home from work. She was grateful to those friends of his, as they had gotten him out of the cottage, and back into the land of the living after Mia's death. Sammy knew that he was not permitted to have Brittany inside of the cottage, alone with him, at any time. And he would be paid an allowance if he agreed to periodically play board games with Syd while Saylor was gone.

The only question Sammy had for his mother was *why do you have to travel for work?* Her response was *something had come up, and she didn't have to, she wanted to.*

*

Saylor left the beach in her jeep before the kids were awake. It was easier that way. She didn't want to feel the guilt, or back out. Max was still asleep in their bed as she stood in their room, dressed and ready to go. She zipped her suitcase shut, and set it in the doorway. She had packed a little bit of everything, mostly casual clothes and swimwear. Nash hadn't told her where they were going. The only plan she was aware of was they were taking her jeep. Neither one of them wanted it to be found parked anywhere, especially not at Nash's condo. It would just be easier to drive it, Nash had suggested. No one would stop by his condo to notice his vehicle in the garage. He had told Max that he was going to paint his condo for a few days, as he and Londyn would most likely opt to sell once their divorce was settled. Saylor assumed Max wouldn't check up on Nash, and she hoped he wouldn't find it strange that she was out of town at the same time he was going to miss days of work. It was a chance, however, they were both willing to take. And it was a risky one.

Saylor drove straight to the condo, before sunrise, to pick up Nash. This was deceit. And this, when Saylor allowed herself to think about it, felt wrong. Even still, she did it.

When she had stood over Max, asleep on his side of the bed, she thought how he was oblivious to what she was about to do, and who she was going to be with for the duration of her trip away from her family. She hated him a little at that moment for not understanding her. For not knowing what she needed

If Things Were Different

from him. And she loathed herself even more for needing a way to keep her head above the water. She was drowning in her marriage, and she only wanted to grab the life preserver that Nash had thrown to her.

She opted not to wake her sleeping husband before she left the cottage. She only walked out of their bedroom and quietly closed the door behind her. And on the table in the kitchen, she left a handwritten note for her family. *Be safe while I'm gone. Love you guys.*

✱

Saylor drove up on Nash's driveway, directly in front of the three-car garage. He certainly lived lavishly. The cottage didn't even have a garage. Even still, she caught herself thinking she would choose the cottage over any place else, any day. That thought caught her off guard for a moment. But it was true.

He put a leather duffle bag in the backseat of her jeep, and told her he would drive, since where they were going was a surprise. Saylor hopped out of the driver's seat, and met him right there at her door before she walked around to the passenger side. "Nervous?" he asked her under the early morning sky.

"Yeah," she admitted, "so let's go. Hurry, before I rethink it." Nash obliged. He hadn't touched her, or kissed her, like he wanted to. There would be all the time in the world for that, for the two of them alone together, the next few days.

The drive was only twenty-one point nine miles, and exactly thirty-three minutes later they had arrived at their destination. Crystal Coast, Harker's Island, North Carolina. They made their way to the private island by ferry. The days ahead of them were going to be spent on an eighty-five mile stretch of crystalline blue water and pearlescent shoreline, where Nash told her they could watch the sun both rise and set into the sparkling Atlantic waters. Time could be spent kayaking along the laced inlets and waterways that zigzagged through the Crystal Coast. There were camping, picnicking and adventure trails that wound throughout the Croatan National Forest. There were diving spots along the Gulf Stream of crystal clear water, where divers could spear fish. The activities there were endless, and Saylor laughed out loud after Nash told her what the next few days could entail for them.

"You're not one to just lie on the beach, are you?" she teased him.

"I figured you could do that at home," he said, halfheartedly, and they were both thrown back to reality. She had a separate life from him. A home. A family.

"You're right," she stated. "I'm just surprised that you planned for us to be a part of such an exciting adventure."

"Don't give me too much credit," he said, "because all I really want to do is take you to bed."

She laughed. It was so comfortable between them that it was frightening. Or at least it could be if she allowed it. She wanted to be with him too. And now they had just walked through the front doorway of one of the private homes dotting the coastline. It reminded her a little of home, her cottage, but only because it was so close to the beach. This place was extravagant and opulent. Everything from the leather furniture to the stainless steel appliances in the full kitchen was top of the line. Saylor thought of her old 1947 vintage gas burning stove in the cottage. It had been her grandmothers and she refused to replace it, even when Max said the appliance store had to special order the repair parts the last time it broke down. Those old, sentimental things made that cottage the cherished home it was for her. For all of them. Saylor was lost in thought as Nash came up behind her, wrapping his arms around her. "Hey, you zoned out on me…"

"I did. Just thinking about how fancy this place is…"

"Let's check out the bedroom," he suggested, as he pulled her by the hand. She dropped her handbag and sunglasses on the granite countertop. And she followed him upstairs. A king-size bed, that looked like she was going to need a stepladder to get up on it, was staring back at them as they entered the doorway. The ceilings were high and arched. Everything was wood. The floors, the walls, and those cathedral ceilings.

"This almost has a cabin feel to it," Saylor stated.

"I like it," Nash replied.

"This feels weird. I'm just going to say it," Saylor admitted. "I have a husband, I have children. I'm lying to them every second I'm gone."

Nash turned her toward him. He touched the base of her chin with two of his fingers. "Remember what happened between us when I said, don't think, just feel?" Saylor nodded, but she felt her eyes get teary. "We have three days. Just feel and do and be with me. And at the end of our stay here together, you can drive your jeep back to your life. I don't want you to choose that, but if you do, I will respect that decision, and move on with my life."

"Are you serious?" Saylor asked him. She thought he would wait for her forever. Fight for her until she gave in — and gave up Max.

"That's not what you want me to do it, is it?" Nash asked her. He knew her all too well. Maybe that's why he had phrased his words the way he did. He knew in his heart that eventually she was going to choose him, and finally they would have a life together. The life that was meant to be theirs.

"We've spent years fighting this, struggling with being apart. So, yeah, I guess I'm a bit taken aback by your willingness to walk away."

Nash took her face in both of his hands. "I'm not going to be willing, but I'll force myself to let you go — if you can't walk away from your life as you've known it. I just want to focus on now. You and me. We're together. We made this happen because we both know that it needs to. Let's worry about the consequences and the final decisions later.

"I like how you think. Make me think that way throughout our stay here. Make me believe it's only us in this small corner of the world. Even if it's only for a little while. There are no guarantees, Nash. We both know that, right?" Saylor was still torn, and confused. But the one thing she knew for certain was she was there with Nash because she wanted to be.

If Things Were Different

Nash pulled her closer and kissed her full on the lips. She responded. Her body limped in his arms when he kissed her like that. It always had, and she knew it always would. They parted, and he spoke. "How am I doing?" Her lips parted into a smile. "You told me to make you think the way I do throughout our stay here." He kissed her again. This time he teased and nibbled on the tip of her tongue. She groaned. She was already convinced, and completely taken in, by him.

They kicked off their sandals. Nash pulled her dress over her head. Saylor removed his shirt above his. He led her over to the bed and lifted her up on it. And then he crawled overtop of her white lacy bra and panty-clad body. She tugged at his khaki shorts, fumbling with the zipper. He undid the clasp in the front of her bra, and cupped her free and full breasts in his hands. This time, it wasn't rushed between them. They weren't in the pitch blackness, down on the floor, during the aftermath of a storm. They weren't as frantically eager to become one before the other changed their mind. This was more about exploring each other again. Taking their time to feel and to see who they were all over again — together, and as one. The years had changed their bodies some. But they still fit together like they were meant to be passionate lovers.

Saylor's body trembled with her release, as Nash settled beside her in the aftermath of ecstasy. No woman before had ever taken him to that point of pleasure and bliss and the sense of true love.

He touched her face, her neck, and he traced his finger on one of her full breasts. She turned to him. She looked satisfied and seductive all at once. Knowing he just *had her* aroused him all over again. "I love you, Saylor. I always have. What I'm saying changes nothing about what I said before. I just need to say it. I love you."

Saylor never hesitated, not even for the slightest moment. "I love you back, Nash Parker." He smiled. His heart felt as if it would boil over. And this time she kissed his lips first. And a moment later their bodies were entangled all over again on that bed, in that private exotic hideaway along the coastline.

And downstairs, on top of the kitchen counter where Saylor left her handbag, her cell phone rang inside of it. Max had already tried to call her twice. This time he chose to leave her a voicemail.

Saylor! Call me back now. It's urgent.

23

A half a day had passed before either of them were ready to tear themselves apart from each other in that bed upstairs. They dressed again in the clothes that were strewn across the floor. And they made their way downstairs to the kitchen, where they both expected to find an empty refrigerator and bare cupboards. Nash was the first one to check regardless, as Saylor reached inside of her handbag for her cell phone. The reality was she would have to check in with her family. They had been under the assumption that she drove five hours away to Charlotte. When really, she was only thirty minutes from the cottage. That lie, and what she and Nash had done upstairs in a borrowed bedroom had also sat like a heavy weight on her chest right now. There were times she could forget everything else, and just be. And then there were the back to reality moments like now.

Her eyes widened as soon as she held the phone in her hand. Three missed calls and one voicemail were all from Max. Nash had said something while bent forward with his head inside of the refrigerator. Saylor never made sense of his words. She only spoke as her heart rate quickened. "Max is trying to get ahold of me…"

Nash pulled back from the refrigerator, and asked, "Just checking in to see if you made it?"

"I don't know. Maybe. He left a voicemail. She then put the message that Max left on speaker.

Saylor! Call me back now. It's urgent.

"Oh my God, Nash. Something's happened!" Saylor felt sick to her stomach. She wasn't that far from home, but she had gone so far from honest and trustworthy.

"Just calm down before you call him back," Nash advised her. "Take a few deep breaths. It's fine. I'm sure everyone is okay."

Saylor nodded her head, hoping with every fiber of her being that he was right. Her guilt though made her feel as if she deserved for something bad to happen. She never should have left her family — and turned to Nash.

Max's phone rang until his voicemail came on. "He's not answering," Saylor told Nash, and the panic rose in her chest. While it was typical for him not to take her calls during his work day, she was alarmed because he had called her. He told her to call him back. *It was urgent.* Saylor immediately called

If Things Were Different

Sammy's cell phone number next. And when his phone also rang too many times, leaving her call unanswered, her fear mounted. "Sammy isn't answering. He's a teenager, his phone never leaves his hand, or his pocket."

"Maybe he's surfing," Nash spoke the first thing he thought of, and then they both felt the sudden sadness of his comment.

"He doesn't surf anymore, he hasn't since the accident," Saylor spoke solemnly. "He could be on the beach with his friends, or swimming, but this is just strange that I can't reach either of them," she sighed, and then spoke what she knew she had to do. "Nash, I have to go back…"

"Wait. They think you're in Charlotte. You can't just call, get no answer, and then run out the door. You'll be back there in less than an hour. How are you going to explain that?"

"I've dug myself in a pretty deep hole here, already," she chided herself. It served her right, she thought. She had lied, and been unfaithful. She would take the wrath though. She just needed to know that her children and Max were safe.

"Hey, stop," Nash walked over to her, stood close, and touched her face with his open palm, and she grasped his wrist. "It's all going to work out. You just have to keep trying to get Max to pick up his damn phone."

Two hours went by. Their luggage was still parked, untouched, just inside the front entrance where they had placed it when they got there. Saylor had not moved from sitting by the kitchen table, with her phone in her hand. Nash convinced her to drink some water, but that was the only thing she touched. He was starving, and he was angry at Max. This was time wasted that he and Saylor could have been spending together, happily. Nash certainly hoped nothing was wrong with any one of them back at the cottage, but a part of him grew angrier at Max. It would be exactly like him to pull a stunt like that, to purposely worry Saylor — if he had somehow found out that they were together. He didn't want to share his theory with Saylor, but he knew he had to.

"I could be wrong about this, but I think you should prepare yourself for something when you do go home," Nash began.

"You think he knows, don't you? He knows we're together."

Nash could have smiled at her right now. They could still read each other's minds, finish sentences before they were completely spoken. This woman belonged with him. "It just doesn't add up. If something was wrong, someone would have answered their phone by now, or tried calling you again. We need to go," Nash said, regretfully. "You need to go back home."

Saylor reached for his hand, and held it in hers for a moment before speaking. "Thank you. I don't want to leave, I don't want to see these wonderful few days never happen. Those few hours we had upstairs weren't enough." Saylor could have cried. *How could something that felt so right be wrong?*

If Things Were Different

"Well that's our story, isn't it? It's never been enough." He wanted to say it was time that they fought the odds and changed that, but he couldn't. Not until Saylor was ready. A part of him actually wished Max knew the truth. But he, like Saylor, also fretted the changes ahead if everything fell apart. He would likely lose his career, his shared position at the helm of the company he and Max built together from the ground up. But, in his mind, he would gain everything if he could have a life with Saylor.

"Drive me to the condo, and I'll go to the cottage from there," she told him, as she stood up near him. He pulled her down on his lap, and forced her to look at him. His hands were on the sides of her face. She lifted up her own hand and brushed back the brown hair hanging wildly above his eyebrows.

"The second we get to Morehead, you are going to have only one thing on your mind. Getting to the cottage. I'm telling you this now so I won't hold you up there. I love you. Reach for me if you need me, and I'll be there." Their lips met with force, and they held on tightly to each other one last time. Saylor squeezed her eyes closed and tears seeped out of the corners as she kissed him hard on the mouth.

This didn't have to be goodbye, but it sure as hell felt like it was for Saylor.

24

The walk, or more like a hard sprint, up that cobblestone sidewalk felt too much like a walk of shame. Only it was still the same day as when Saylor left, so she clearly could be wearing the same clothes. The shameful part was she had sex with another man and it was hardly impromptu. It was preplanned, and Saylor had intentionally lied to her family in order to go away, alone, with Nash.

When Saylor reached the porch of the cottage, she noticed the front window blinds were drawn. They were never closed, unless Max was home and a storm was coming. That always annoyed her. Especially because he knew how much she loved watching storms moving in and wreaking havoc. She pushed open the front door, and stepped inside. Everything was still in the jeep, her suitcase, her handbag, and her phone. She left it all in there when she parked next to Max's truck. He was there.

If Things Were Different

All she carried was her key ring with the jeep and cottage keys. "Max?" she called out, and she moved toward the window to twist the wand to open the blinds. It was dark in there. It was as if the world outside had been shut out, and she was trapped inside. Little did she know, that was his intention.

"Keep those closed."

Saylor turned around at the sound of his voice from across the room. "Max? What the hell is going on? You called me, you said it was urgent that I call you back, and then you never answered your phone!" Her initial thought as she spoke was *Nash had been right. There was no emergency. Max had pulled this stunt to get her home. Which also meant that he knew she had lied to him.*

"You got here fast for being in Charlotte, five hours away," Max's eyes were cold. Saylor didn't have to assume anymore. She had been found out.

"I got here as quickly as I could," she answered as vaguely as she could. "What is wrong? Where are the kids?"

"Our kids are fine. They'll be home later after we sort out a few things," Max stated as a matter of fact, and Saylor prepared herself for the fight of her life. She only wondered at this point if she was going to fight for him and their marriage, or fight for her freedom. "I found it odd that Nash was going to take a few days off of work at the same time you had to suddenly go out of town for a job that you have never once traveled for. I believed you though. It was Nash's story that planted doubt in my head." Saylor remained standing near the closed window blinds, and Max stayed stationary clear across the room. "I tracked your phone to Harker's Island. You two didn't go too far, just far enough, huh? I considered letting three days go by, but I couldn't stand the thought of you spending those nights with him." Saylor cringed at the fact of her and Nash already having shared a bed. She wondered if Max believed his timing had stopped them from being intimate.

"So you purposely worried me?" Saylor finally spoke. She wasn't going to deny this, or be submissive to him. She would face what she did. She had no other choice. "You had me thinking the worst could have happened to one of the kids, or you!"

"I wanted you to come home," Max spoke in answer. "This cottage is ours. Our family lives here. You belong here, Saylor."

"That's just it," she swallowed hard so she would not cry. "I don't know that for sure anymore." That was an admission to herself right now, as well as to Max. "Hear me out before you react." Max stayed silent as she continued. "When you came into my life as a man who wanted to help me get over Nash, I wanted to love you the way I loved him. And yes, I wanted you to help me forget him. I looked for the day that you could make me do that. We got married. We had babies. We made a life together on this beautiful beach. But something has always been missing for me. You've thrown Nash and me, along with Londyn, together time and again for work and social things. Mia was such a huge part of our lives. There were always boundaries and Nash and I respected them. So much changed though when Mia died… and then Londyn left. You were right, he was free, and he wanted me." Saylor watched Max clench his jaw. "But it's not just Nash who's at fault. I've harbored such deep feelings for him for so long. And I gave in. Right or wrong, I've been back in his bed."

Max made tense fists with both of his hands. Saylor wondered if he was about to punch the wall, or slam down on a tabletop. "Are you leaving me, Saylor? Are the two of you going to rekindle what you think you had for a ridiculously short time, two decades ago?" Max was mocking them. Of course he would, because he was angry and Saylor could never expect him to understand that she loved Nash then — and now. It was unfair of her to think that he could.

"I can't answer that, Max. Not yet." That was the most honest answer Saylor could give him. Yes, she was at a crossroad, and she had no idea where she would eventually turn.

"I respect that," he told her, and she listened raptly. "If you're torn, that means I still have a chance."

"Are you saying that you can forgive me?" Saylor bluntly asked him.

"I think that will take some time," he admitted. "But I have loved you all these years knowing that you loved him. Nothing's changed for me in that regard. I just never thought you would cross the line with him. You are my wife."

"A part of me wants to run to you right now and swear to you that I'm yours and I'll never be unfaithful again." Saylor was exceptionally calm. "But that's only a part of me. And you don't deserve that, Max. I can't be who you need me to be anymore. I've tried, but I can't. I want to see the kids now. I need to begin to prepare them for the changes. I want to have more open and honest discussions with you until we can figure this all out. I don't know how to part ways, and if we do, I'll still need you to co-parent with me the way we have always done."

"I know what I deserve, Saylor," Max spoke adamantly, in reference to Saylor's previous comment. "You are the only woman for me. I'll excuse your indiscretions. I just want our life back. I want you to stop this unreasonable talk about leaving and living separate lives." Saylor's eyes widened. This was almost eerie to her. They were standing there in a dark room. Max was acting completely out of character. *He was her husband. He should be angry with her. And screaming and yelling. She cheated on him. She broke her marriage vows. And she already insinuated that she still wanted to be with Nash.* Yet Max's only focus was on things staying the same.

"I keep hearing what you just said to me, and the strange part of it is, I don't think you are hearing me," Saylor began. "You will excuse my indiscretions? Max, I'm not some whore looking to have sex with just anyone. I'm in love with Nash. I've never stopped loving him." Her words for him were harsh, but she was clearly offended by what he had said to her first. She had never gotten over Nash. The two of them had denied their feelings for far too long. This was about a lost love, not just sex outside of marriage.

"Oh I hear you," Max retaliated. His anger had surfaced. "You will always love him. Got it. But you're my wife. And you're going to tell Nash that you've decided to stay married to me."

If Things Were Different

Since when did Max, the often ball-less husband of hers, make demands? The hurt and embarrassment had changed him. He was now all at once callous and courageous.

"Are you trying to force me to do that?" she boldly asked him, as she stepped toward him. She had enough of this space and weirdness between them. And, quite frankly, she was not at all used to seeing Max this way.

"Force? No." Saylor just now noticed that he was wearing a black polo shirt and black dress shorts. That was the look she liked on him. But, right now, he only looked *dark* to her, as in sinister and chilling. "You can't walk out on me and our family."

"I'm not leaving the kids," Saylor spoke in no uncertain terms.

"We are a packaged deal, that's what a family is," Max replied.

Saylor softened a little. This was the Max she had known and loved. "We're both going to need time to accept this, to get used to the idea. Why don't we just take the kids out to dinner, or grill and hang out here on the beach? We can talk about this after we sleep on it, and have a little more time to process it all." *Not that Saylor would be able to sleep.*

"I don't want to pretend to be a family, I want to continue to be one," Max hung his head, and his words instantly saddened her. This was again a glimpse back to the man she was married to. He was plain and simple and he only wanted what he already had. Nothing more. Guilt settled in her mind and heart again. She was the reason they would no longer be *a family*. She was going to tear apart their lives, the lives both Sammy and Syd only knew them to be. This was suddenly killing her. *Saylor wanted Nash, but at what cost?*

Max finally conceded. "The kids are about a mile down on the beach. Brittany's parents are renting a cottage this summer. Sammy and Syd took a walk there with her." Saylor nodded. She felt relieved that they were close by. For a moment she had feared Max would try to keep their children from her. And that would be a fight he was sure to lose. But right now, Saylor recognized that Max was only fighting to keep her. He was obviously scared to lose her, and she was just as fearful to walk away as she had been all along.

25

All evening, around their children, it was life as normal for their family of four. They ate dinner together, and Max stayed at the cottage with them afterward. He had missed most of the day of work, and never mentioned going back to catch up. When Sammy joined his friends on the beach at dusk, Saylor helped Syd with her bath and then tucked her into bed. This was the moment she was not looking forward to all night. She and Max would be alone again. They could no longer pretend that all was well. They were going to have to talk about it, *about them*, again.

After Syd was tucked into bed and quickly drifting off to sleep, Saylor made her way to the living room where Max was lying on the sofa. He was flipping through the channels on the TV when she walked in. She was going to sit down in the armchair adjacent to him, but he bent his legs and offered her a spot at his feet. She sat down there on the sofa.

"Do you wish you were still with him?" Max asked her outright, referring to what would still have been their romantic getaway if he had not interfered. *And what was she supposed to say? What did he expect her to say?* The two of them had not even been on the island for more than a few hours together, and they had spent most of their time in each other's arms. It was both familiar and comfortable as well as new and exciting with Nash. Being with Max, everything was routine and expected. *But what did she imagine it would be after fifteen years together?* They had gotten into a groove together. It wasn't terrible. It was her life. Their life. Saylor had reached the point where she was torn. Maybe she had always been that way. Only it had been so much simpler when Nash wasn't an option. Only a what if. A lost dream. A fantasy. The reality of what she had done to Max hit her hard today once she returned to the cottage, and she was reeling from it. To answer his blunt question right now was almost too much for her. But she tried.

"I don't know," were the first words out of her mouth. She didn't over think. She just spoke. "I see my life here as comfortable and habitual. Our kids are happy and healthy. We are productive and successful in our careers. And yes, we live on the beach. How amazing is that?" Saylor paused. Max continued to lie there as she sat at the base of his bent legs and bare feet. "And then I think of what might have been if Londyn had not been pregnant, and if Nash and I had gotten our chance. *What if things were different* has hung over our heads, and lingered on our minds for years. The wilder side of me wants to run and see where that life with him takes me. But, the woman in me that you know, the person who errs on the side of caution and plays it safe, is the one who doesn't want to hurt you more than I already have. I don't want to uproot our children's lives. I don't want to make a mistake. I know that I have a choice to make. I can stay here and resume being content, but always wondering. Or I can leave and see if the grass is really greener over there."

Max sat up, and he sat shoulder to shoulder with her. He looked straight ahead. And after he was silent for a really long time, he said, "We don't have any grass. We're all sand outside."

Saylor smiled, and turned her body to face him. "Yeah, and you know how much I love the sand between my toes."

"Enough to keep you here?" Max asked, finally turning to look at her beside him. She was close to him. He was dying to reach her. Not so much physically. He just hoped to touch her heart.

"Max…" Saylor waited a few seconds before she again spoke her honest thoughts. "When I first got here today, you were making it pretty easy for me to want to walk away. I was angry that you had tricked me into coming home. I was ashamed that you had known what I'd done. All of my emotions were telling me to run out of that door — straight to a new life."

"And now?" he asked. He'd be lying to himself if he didn't believe Saylor was rethinking her so-called chance with Nash.

"I need to talk to Nash. I know how awful that makes me seem. Jesus, Max. Just kick me out for being such a selfish bitch. It would make this decision so much easier." Saylor choked on a sob, and Max turned to her, and thumbed the tear that made its way down her cheek.

"Then talk to him," Max said, surprising Saylor and himself too actually. "But remember who he is. And don't think I do not know that man. I've grown up with him. I run a company with him. What you're going to get with Nash Parker is excitement, and fly-by-the-seat-of-your-pants moments that will make your head spin. It's wildly attractive and such a draw for a man to be the way he is. I've been taken in by him too. I oftentimes have wished I had more of what he has. I've told you as much. He may be bolder, more of a charmer and a risk-taker than I am. But, with all of my faults and everything that I lack compared to him in my mind, and yours, I would never take another man's wife. My best friend's wife. It's just wrong, Saylor. It's fucking wrong. So remember one thing. If Nash is capable of hurting me, and so swiftly writing off his wife of almost twenty years, what will stop him one day from breaking your heart?"

26

The one thing Saylor never thought she would be was pulled in two different directions. All those years ago, the decision had been made for her. She couldn't be with Nash. So she chose Max. Now, she wanted to be with Nash and that door was essentially wide open for her to walk through. It was the door to her life with Max that she didn't know if she could close. He loved her. He was a good man. He promised her forever and he meant it with is body, mind, and soul. And she loved him too. Just not in the same way she had loved Nash. One fact that continued to weigh on her mind was the passion and love from their once upon a time love story — and was it going to be worth all that she would leave behind? She wanted to believe that it would be.

Her cell phone had five separate messages from Nash when she finally powered it on in the middle of the night. Rain was sprinkling down, as Saylor sat under the protective overhang on the front porch. Nash was, by right, worried about her. With each message, his desperation seemed to increase.

You okay?

Max knows, doesn't he?

I assumed there was no emergency when I drove by and saw both of your vehicles, and the cottage was well lit.

Jesus, Saylor. I can't stand this. Text me. Call me. Meet me.

I'll be up all night. Reach out.

Saylor wanted to call him, to hear his voice. But she didn't want to risk waking her family, so she sent Nash her first response to him in hours.

Max knows. He's hurt. But — he still wants me to choose him. I need to see you. I need you to hear me. I'm torn. I love you, I've always loved you, but my life with my family is holding me back from taking a definite chance on us.

A few minutes later, Nash responded.

He's a forgiving man, Nash said on Max's behalf. *I'm not so sure I could swallow my pride that way. I think my need to see you is greater. Tomorrow?*

That admission stuck with Saylor for longer than she wanted it do. Had she completely overlooked Max's goodness and his strengths and his gifts to her in those ways through the years?

If Things Were Different

And you're a patient man. Tomorrow at noon? Your condo? She assumed lunchtime would be ideal for him to break away. They didn't have to sneak around, or find the right time. Max already knew she wanted and needed to speak to Nash. It still felt wrong and deceitful to her though.

I'll be there.

✱

Before Saylor could ring the bell, Nash opened the door to let her in. And when the door was closed behind them, they fell into each other's arms. They kissed with desperation. Touched with desire. It didn't feel like *hello, I've missed you.* It felt too much like a *goodbye* they were both resisting.

It could have gone farther. Nash could have carried her upstairs to bed. Saylor could have begged him to take her right there on the hardwood floor. *Obviously, it wouldn't have been the first time.*

But they both mustered the strength within to pull away.

Saylor spoke to him first. "I need to talk this out, I want to say the words out loud to make sense of this. To decode what I'm doing with my life. And to understand how to keep myself from hurting those I love, and finally being true to myself."

Nash knew what her decision was going to be. He saw it in her eyes, and he sensed it from her soul when she was in his arms. And that's why she had to allow him to speak first. He wanted her to have a change of heart from what she came there to tell him. But she spoke so suddenly, before he could ask her not to.

"I have so many reasons to keep my family intact," Saylor began, already with tears spilling over her eyes, "but only one to walk away, to begin something new but so incredibly familiar to my heart. Nash, you're the wind in my sail. You've always been. We owe it to each other to chance this, to seize what might have been if fate hadn't twisted things up for us so long ago. There's a reason we've remained connected and so engaged in each other's lives. That alone created a means for us to fall back into each other so effortlessly. Do this with me, Nash."

She saw the tears in his eyes before he spoke to her. "I've waited half my life to be able to reach for you again," he swallowed hard the lump building up in his throat before he continued on. "Loving you is a part of who I am. Loving each other has made us who we are, even as we've been apart for so damn long. To know that you chose me — you chose us — makes me love you even more." Saylor anticipated that Nash would reach for her, close the space between them, and initiate their love making. She wanted him. She chose him. For the rest of their lives. "I would never purposely hurt you, Saylor. I know that I broke your heart once, and I know mine completely shattered. It all but killed me to let you go then, and it feels a million times more painful now."

Saylor didn't understand his implication. *He was letting her go? Why? No! She couldn't withstand that kind of pain again.* She was wide-eyed and trembling now, as she waited for him to clarify what she believed she misinterpreted.

"Sammy was here last night," Nash told her.

Saylor was confused. "He was at the beach with his friends…"

"No, he came to see me. He walked here from the beach."

"My God, does he know about us?" Her son was a teenager. He would never understand the depth of this. He would think less of her. She would be a whore in his eyes. No boy should ever have to think of his mother in that way.

Nash nodded. "Max told him. He's a perceptive kid. I'm sure he cornered Max."

"Stop it. Do not defend Max for this. He never should have told Sammy about us!" Saylor was angry and ashamed. She didn't want her son to find out that way. And Max had kept that from her. She immediately assumed that was his way of retaliating at her for her betrayal.

"Hear me out," Nash stated. "Sammy came to me to clear the air. He's a deep thinker, like his mother, and he had something on his mind."

"He asked you to back off, didn't he?" Saylor covered her hand over her mouth, trying to stifle a sob.

"In so many words, yes. Saylor, he shared with me how he and Mia used to talk about us. They knew of our love story because I confided in Mia, and in turn Mia told Sammy." Saylor had known that Mia was aware of the history they shared. She remembered Mia's words to her not so long ago.

What you did... for me... and for my parents to be together as a family with me... was selfless. It was as if she had understood her father's unbreakable bond with Saylor. *My dad told me that sometimes there's a cosmic pull between two people. You can't ignore it, and even when you try to, you're still going to be drawn together like gravity. He said that he believes in fate having a way of circling back over the paths that we are meant to cross.*

"Our kids apparently had the discussion of what if their parents had not gotten together, and how that would mean the two of them would not exist. They praised Londyn and Max for their separate roles in all of our lives," Nash explained.

"It's natural, it's a given for kids to want their parents to be together," Saylor interrupted and there was a panic in her voice. *A fifteen year old was not going to decide their future! Even if he was her son.*

"It's more than that," Nash added. "Mia believed I was a better man, much better than how I am behaving now. Sammy told me what she hoped for, regarding us — and the lives that would be greatly affected if we were ever together." Saylor listened to his every word, but at the same time she was afraid to hear more. "Mia believed in fate, but she also believed in kindness and loyalty and doing the right thing. She said I had instilled all of that in her. She admired and respected me... but I'm not so sure she would now." Nash stopped talking. The pain of losing Mia was still incredibly raw. He was beginning to believe that his grief had clouded his moral judgment when he chose to pursue Saylor as if no one else mattered. Not Londyn. Not Max. And not the children, including his daughter.

If Things Were Different

"She would have understood eventually," Saylor responded, trying to be compassionate and respectable of the fact that Mia was gone. It still pained her too in the worst way. *That beautiful soul was never coming back.* "Sammy tried to convince you to give me up, because he wants his family to stay together. Of course he loves his dad, he doesn't want to see Max get hurt. But Nash… this is us, this is our chance." There was desperation in her voice. Hearing of Sammy's efforts had touched Saylor, and she knew she was going to have a long road with her son, working toward his forgiveness and understanding. One day, perhaps when he's a man, Saylor was confident that Sammy would understand.

Nash stepped closer to her, as he attempted to blink back his tears. "I can't be a man that Mia wouldn't be proud of."

Tears were clouding Saylor's eyes now. "No. Please. Please. No." Nash was breaking her heart all over again. Just like that they were back on the beach nineteen years ago, and he was telling her he could not be with her. They could not be together. Only this time it hurt more. It pained her deeper than she could handle. She had risked so much to be with him. And she truly believed he was worth it all.

She reached for him, she held his face in both of her hands. She brushed back his hair from his forehead. She wiped away the tears on his cheeks with her fingers. He held her, low around her waist, and pulled her closer to his body.

"We can't." Nash spoke with serious regret in his voice. This choice, his choice, was absolutely unbearable.

Saylor cried harder at the words she never thought she would hear from him again. Not after how intensely he pursued her and fought for her. For them. And especially not after how much he loved her. No one had ever made her feel so needed, so wanted.

"I cannot believe Sammy changed your mind," she cried.

"He didn't. He was just the messenger. It was Mia," Nash stated. "It was how she felt. I have to honor her memory. This is my sign to do what is right, just like I did the day she was born."

Saylor nodded. "It's not like I don't understand. It just hurts too much." Once again, she had felt like a life-changing decision had been made for her. Just once, she wanted to have the final say. *This was her life!* But deep down in her soul, she knew her final choice, the choice that she so desperately had wanted to make this time, would hurt too many people.

He held her close, and he kissed her lips one last time. Neither one of them had a handle on their tears when they parted from each other's arms.

"I don't know how I'll be able to stand to see you around," Saylor choked back a sob.

"I've given that some thought." Nash knew it would be too painful, and that there was no way he could do it either. "I told Max this morning that I am taking a leave of absence for one year. I need to get out of this city and the company for awhile. He agreed to reconvene with me once I return. There's a real possibility that I'll sell my share of M&N someday."

If Things Were Different

Saylor shook her head. So many changes had engulfed their lives in recent months. First, they lost Mia. Then, Londyn left. And finally, she and Nash had turned to each other. And now he was leaving. "Where will you go?"

Nash smiled a little. "LA." And then it dawned on her. Londyn had signed a one-year contract to model in California. Nash was going after her.

"Londyn," Saylor spoke in what was barely a whisper. Jealousy had not surfaced in her heart. It could have, if she'd let it. But she knew the two of them had shared more than just a daughter. And maybe it was finally time for Nash to appreciate that. "Do you think she will take you back?"

"I don't know," Nash admitted. "I wouldn't blame her if she tossed me out the minute I arrived. I don't deserve her love or forgiveness, but second chances sometimes have to begin with the bare bones. We build those kinds of things back up, and earn them all over again."

"Sounds like Max and me," Saylor acknowledged.

"Maybe we can both be better partners to them because of what we've had between us? It's time we put our heart and soul into them, instead of the memories of us, and the what-might-have-been possibilities with each other." Nash had a viable point, and Saylor wanted to take it to heart. But, right now, this all hurt too much.

"I want you to be happy, Nash," Saylor began speaking what she knew she needed to say to him. "I want you to live a life with no regrets, and I hope I can, too. A part of me wants to tell you that if you ever change your mind, I'll be sitting under the stars at the red cottage on the beach. But that's not fair to either of us. So instead, I'm telling you goodbye. I love you beyond words. And I always will. But this time, I'm letting you go." Saylor was crying too hard to continue to look up at him now. Nash lifted her chin with two of his fingers and he kissed her face and finally her lips before she heard him say that he loved her more. But he never said goodbye.

27

Saylor was back at the beach. She sat behind the wheel of her jeep for the longest time. She wasn't out of tears, but she continued to will herself not to cry.

After she finally did get out and walk up to the cottage, she was on the cobblestone path when she looked toward the water, and she saw Sammy walking up the shore with his surfboard tucked underneath one arm. She was so surprised that, for a moment, she questioned if who she saw was really her son. And then he lifted one hand and waved to her.

She made a sound that was a cross between a laugh and a choked sob. And she waved at him in return. She got off of the sidewalk, kicked off her sandals, and stepped into the sand as she walked toward her boy. He was smiling when she reached him.

"Sam? Did you really?" He nodded. "Why now?"

"I did it for Mia, mom." Saylor was so proud of him that she reached out and pulled his wet self into a tight hug. She didn't care if her white sundress was now soaked down the front.

"She was so loved," Saylor spoke, thinking of what Nash had done — what he had given up — also for Mia. Sammy stayed near her, but he was silent.

"You know where I've been," she assumed, and he only shrugged his broad, bare shoulders with water dripping off of them. "I don't expect you to understand, not yet," Saylor told him, "but I just want you to know that you were heard."

She watched his lip quiver before he spoke. "Mia understood, and she tried to help me see things the way she did. She wanted you and Nash to stay in the past though. And that's what I told him."

"I know, honey," Saylor mothered him.

"So are you staying, mom? With dad, and Syd and me?" There was such innocence in his question. He didn't sound like a teenager whose voice had deepened last year. He was her little boy again, asking her to stay. One day, Saylor hoped he would understand that she never had any intention of leaving him and his sister. That was never an option. She would always be their mother.

This time Saylor nodded.

"God, I'm so thankful for that!" Sammy's face lit up and he smiled wide.

"And I'm grateful for you, and Syd… and your dad." Just as Saylor said those words, she looked up at the cottage and saw him sitting there on the top step in his red swim trunks and a black t-shirt. She could tell from a distance that his hair was wet. He was the reason their son had finally conquered the waves again. That was just another blessing Max had given her.

"I'll hang out on the beach for a little while, and dry in the sun," Sammy offered, and Saylor gathered how that was his way of giving her and Max time to talk.

When she reached the steps to the cottage, she sat down beside Max on the top one. Saylor wasn't sure how much she wanted to share with him right now. He already knew that Nash was leaving for at least one year, which meant he had hope for Saylor to return to him and their family.

"You don't have to say anything," he spoke, surprising Saylor with his compassion. "All I want to know is if you are here to stay."

Saylor reached for his hand, and he intertwined her fingers with his. When she looked at him at this defining moment, she saw the man who wanted to save her from heartache all those years ago. And this time she was finally ready to let him. "I'm home, Max."

28

Londyn was staying at The Beverly Hills Hotel. Nash already had her contact information. He knew she was living a life of luxury for the year that she relocated to Los Angeles. He believed Londyn deserved it, after all she had been through. He wondered if she was lonely, or if she had gotten back into the dating scene already. That would be easy for her to do as a striking beauty among some of the top models in Hollywood. Nash surprised himself when he felt jealous at the thought of Londyn moving on. And then he chided himself for it. He couldn't justify those emotions. He had not earned them. Not yet anyway.

If Things Were Different

When his flight landed, he took an Uber to the hotel. It was nine o'clock at night. He contemplated booking a room and looking up Londyn in the morning. And then he thought maybe she wasn't even back at the hotel for the night yet. She could be at a function, on the party scene. It was still early in that sense. Nash imagined her in a sleek black dress with a high slit up the side to reveal one of her long legs. He did book a room at the main desk, and then he took the elevator up to the floor that housed the suite Londyn was staying in. He took a chance. That's what this was about. Taking a chance, and hoping for a second chance. This was crazy, so off the wall that he could hardly believe it himself. Nash wanted his wife back. It wouldn't be the same life they had shared, and without Mia every day would bring continued reminders and pain, but maybe between the two of them it could be better.

Nash knocked twice, and waited.

He couldn't tell if there was light or movement behind that large heavy door. He knocked again, and waited longer. Little did he know that Londyn had used the peep hole to see who was on the other side of her door. And she stood there for an entire ninety seconds before she reacted. She considered not answering, not letting him step through that doorway. That was the threshold to her new life. Her life that no longer included him. He had no reason to be there, but that was the thing with Nash. Londyn always wanted to know what he needed, what he wanted, and what was on his mind. She loved everything about him. And probably always will.

She turned the deadbolt, and finally reached for the door handle.

And there he stood. A few inches taller than her at the moment, because she was in bare feet. He wore jeans and a white t-shirt, and boat shoes sans socks. And his hair was shorter. *Nash Parker had actually gotten a haircut.* It was considerably shorter than she had ever seen him have it.

"Nash, what are you doing here?" was her only question. He looked at her. Londyn's long dark hair was hanging loose on her shoulders. She was wearing a short black silk robe, tied around her hourglass waist. She had no makeup on her face, and she looked prepped for bed.

"I was afraid I would wake you… or I thought you could be out for the night," he told her, from the place where he still remained out in the hallway.

"I feel like I should invite you in, but only because I'm standing in my open doorway half naked, and you did come all this way for a reason that peaks my curiosity." Londyn's sense of humor tickled him. *Had he ever truly appreciated her honest wit?* Nash thought of how Mia had been the very same way. He laughed so often with her. And now he missed that terribly, too.

Nash closed the door behind him after she allowed him to come inside. The suite she rented was massive. He could see the king-size bed against the far wall, a small kitchen, and even a hot tub near a set of white double doors that he assumed led to a full bath.

There was also a white leather sectional, which reminded Nash of the two matching sofas in their living room back home at the condo. Londyn sat down on one end of that sectional now, as she crossed one of her long bare legs over the other. "You can sit," she invited him.

"I'd rather stand," he told her, and she knew he would answer that. Whenever Nash had something to say, something that weighed on his mind, he preferred to stand — or pace. She, of course, knew him well.

"Okay, tell me why you're here," she stated, and Nash stared at her for a long few seconds. He had missed her voice. And just being in her presence. She was almost always even-keeled. She had the capability to bring people a sense of calm. He never focused on that before. He never appreciated a lot of things about her before. *What a damn fool.*

"I should have called, I know, to warn you that I was coming. It was spur of the moment, and I guess I didn't want you to tell me not to come. I wasn't going to offer you the chance to turn me away. Not until you at least hear what I have to say." Londyn remained quiet and still, but he had her attention. *He always had.*

"When you left," he began, "I turned to Saylor. Just as you predicted." Londyn did not flinch. She was not at all surprised. "We wanted a life together, even at the expense of her marriage, and her children having a broken home. Saylor was torn, but she really wanted to take a chance on me, on us. We never got that chance all those years ago, and we will not get it now either."

Londyn looked confused. "Did she back out?" Londyn's first thought was Saylor had broken his heart this time. And now he was running back to her. *Like hell if she would be second* best again. *And, really, why would he come back to her? Nash Parker could have any woman he wanted. Well, maybe not his one and only Saylor — if she had inevitably turned him away.*

"No, I did."

"Why?" Londyn was having a difficult time sitting still on the end of the sofa. None of what Nash just said had made any sense at all. She left believing he and Saylor would fall back together and live their happy ever after, despite everyone.

"Mia." One word. Their daughter's name. That's all it took for Londyn to lose her composure. She had not spoken her name, or heard it in the weeks that she had arrived at her new, temporary home. And here he stood. Her husband. And the mere mention of their beautiful child, who had grown into an exceptional young woman, had brought her to tears. "She believed I was a better man. I can't let her down."

Londyn allowed the tears to spill over, as she spoke. "She loved her daddy." Nash nodded, and she could see the tears in his eyes when she looked up at him.

"I have no right to come crawling back to you. I've been a good father, but not a good husband. I don't know how else to ask you this, other than to just say it. I want us to have a second chance. We can build something from the ground up, something better. Not that it will ever be better without our girl, but I only mean better between us. Londyn, tell me I'm not thinking crazy."

She dried her tears with the floppy sleeve of her robe before she spoke to him. "First, you're hardly crawling because you're still on your feet." *Honest wit*, he thought, and he smiled.

If Things Were Different

And then he humored her, and he dropped to his knees on the carpet in front of that sectional. She let out a slight giggle. And hearing that made his insides flutter. "Nash, in all seriousness, we are living different lives now. I'm here, you're there."

She hadn't told him no. Nash was always encouraged when a woman didn't shut him down on his first try.

"I'm actually here," he replied, and she needed more of an explanation from him. "I took a year's leave of absence from M&N. Max agreed. I have to sort out my life before I can ever go back, if I ever go back. Maybe I'm meant to start fresh somewhere else. Maybe it's the only way to move on."

"And you think I am a means for you to start fresh? We are hardly strangers, Nash. The last time I checked, we are married with a divorce pending." Londyn was again searching for answers. She wasn't at all convinced that they were what each other needed anymore.

"I think that sometimes two people need to fall apart in order to realize how much they need each other. I can offer you more this time. I know I can."

"You want me to fall back into a life with you?" Londyn asked him. A part of her right now had come alive again. She had not felt this hopeful since they lost Mia. Nash nodded his head, and dramatically scooted toward her on his knees. She suppressed a giggle this time.

"Yes, I want that so much. What do you say, Mrs. Parker? Give me a year to prove myself worthy to be your husband, a real tried and true husband this time."

"You were always tried and true," she told him, and she meant it. He was never untrustworthy or unreliable. He was their provider. Mia and Londyn had struck gold blessings when they got him. She only wanted him to love her the fiery and fierce way that she knew Nash was capable of loving a woman.

"And you always loved me way more than I ever deserved," he told her, and he meant it. He reached for her with his open palms. And Londyn never hesitated to put her hands in his.

"I do love you," she told him first, as she always had.

Nash lunged forward and he met his lips with hers. Londyn instantaneously responded to him. He did love her, but he would wait before he said it back. He wanted to prove it to her first.

Epilogue

ONE YEAR LATER

The conference room at M&N Solar Energy Development was completely empty — with the exception of two men. The owners. Max wore his standard flat front khakis and red polo shirt with the M&N logo. Nash showed up in jeans and a t-shirt.

They shook hands and sat down. Max wanted no interruptions so he asked Nash to meet him in the conference room where he also had set up a digital presentation to bring Nash up to date with the happenings in their company in the last year. The two men had not been in touch at all.

"I don't know what your plans are," Max started out, "obviously that's why we are meeting today. But regardless, I want to share with you what's been going on here while you've been gone." Nash nodded. "We've held steady," Max explained, showing Nash the numbers, "but we have not grown since you left. I'm not going to beg you. I will buy you out if you're not interested in coming back. I just wanted you to see proof that this company, our company needs you at the helm." This was Max's olive branch. This was his way of forgiving Nash, and letting him know that he missed having him by his side in business — despite everything.

If Things Were Different

Nash was flattered, but more so he was touched by Max's ability to love over hate. Of course Max hated what Nash did with Saylor. But he exemplified in spades that he knew how to man up and move on.

"I do have a plan for my life, now that the fun's over in LA," he smiled. "Londyn's modeling contract is up, and she's decided not to renew it even though there was a really generous offer involved."

Max was happy to know that Nash and Londyn had found their way back to each other. He certainly knew what it felt like to begin again with the woman he loved. "So is Londyn through with modeling altogether?" Max was making conversation that he assumed would lead to Nash's decision about staying with their company, or leaving.

"She says her face is already too bloated to continue on with the skincare company," Nash responded, and Max frowned.

"What the hell does that mean? I've never seen a bloated part of Londyn in all the years I've known her." Max chuckled, and thought, *women!*

"You don't remember when she was pregnant, and her face puffed out like the Michelin man?" Nash held his laugh as he waited to see if Max had caught on.

"What? Are you serious?" Max had definitely understood. "You're having a baby?"

"I'm not, she is... well I planted the seed and all." This time Nash laughed out loud. Max slapped him on the back, and it felt like old times between them again.

"Congratulations, buddy! That's amazing news!" And it was. It was, for many reasons, because a baby had symbolized a new beginning. But most of all, it was a way for Nash and Londyn to have a family again. They were both forty years old. It was more than possible as they had quickly found out once Nash had his vasectomy reversed. There was a time when Londyn didn't want any more children. Her body could not take the changes if she didn't want to risk seeing an end to her modeling career. Time and circumstances had changed her mind. And before it was too late, they made it happen. They were going to be a family of three again.

"So I told you the good news first," Nash stated, and Max tensed a bit. *Nash was leaving the company, and Max would have to press on without him. His absence would go from temporary to permanent.*

"And the bad news?" Max jumpstarted this.

"It doesn't have to be bad news, I guess it just depends on how you look at it," Nash teased. "We've decided to come back and raise another child right here. And if you'll have me back at this company, I would like to return."

"This company is *our* company," Max stated as a matter of fact. "Welcome back, man." And the simple handshake that followed had never meant so much.

If Things Were Different

※

One of their children had a play date down the beach and the other, with a brand new driver's license in his wallet, was cruising the town in a borrowed jeep with his girlfriend in the passenger seat beside him. Sammy was hardly a child anymore. At sixteen, he was for sure enjoying a new kind of freedom. And his parents were savoring some time alone in the cottage.

Saylor laughed as she propped herself up on one elbow in the bed she shared with her husband. It was the middle of the day and she had been hard at work on a prospective grant when Max arrived at home unexpectedly. He pulled her inside from the front porch and they took advantage of their newfound passion. Those stolen moments with each other had become so cherished — and the spontaneity of it was exciting and fun, as Saylor told him time and again.

"What are you eighteen again?" she teased her naked husband beside her. He had become a more attentive lover, and he had just taken her twice in one afternoon. "Careful, flattery will get you a third." She laughed out loud and he grinned at his wife. She was the love of his life.

"I have something to tell you," he began, and he kept his smile.

She pulled up the navy blue sheet to cover her bare lower half. And then Max moved it back down so he could see all of her. She giggled at the thought of him being turned on by her *again*.

"Nash is coming back to M&N." Just the mention of his name caused Saylor to immediately lose her smile. She was completely caught off guard.

"He is? Have you talked to him in person or just from LA?" Saylor didn't know what else to ask that would be appropriate. She wondered time and again if Nash and Londyn had been able to save their marriage. She knew he had relocated to LA for a year, but she had not known if they were together.

"He's home. They are home. I met with him this morning at the office."

"They? Londyn's with him?" Saylor hoped for that to be true.

"Yeah, and soon they will be a party of three again."

"What?" Saylor felt her heart fill with immense joy. She thought of Mia. She thought of Nash as being a daddy again. And she imagined how blessed Londyn must feel to be given the chance to be a mother again. "They're pregnant?"

Max nodded and smiled.

"I'm really happy for them," Saylor wanted Max to know that.

"I know you are," he told her.

"I love you, Max. Nothing changes when Nash returns. You got that?"

"Oh I disagree," Max stated. "Everything changes. For the better. We are all better for our time apart."

If Things Were Different

Saylor agreed, and she slid her body closer to her husband. She touched him first, and they both hoped that Sammy had a full tank of gas to keep him jeepin' for a little while longer.

✱

That same day Saylor was in for another shock. She received a text from Londyn, asking her to meet at the condo. Her first instinct was to politely bow out of the invitation. It was inappropriate, considering the last time Londyn had summoned both her and Nash there. She had practically pushed them together then. Not that they needed a shove in each other's direction. But then Saylor remembered Max's words to her just hours ago. *Everything had changed for the better. And they were all better because of the time and space.*

Saylor confirmed that she would be there. And then Londyn asked her to meet in the backyard. That seemed odd, but Saylor wondered if it would just be too difficult to be in the same exact space as they had been the fateful day of the storm and the brutally honest revelations in that living room.

Londyn had been alone when Saylor arrived outside. She was standing far out, at the perimeter of their land, near that massive, old, white oak tree. Saylor traipsed through the tall grass, which pricked her bare feet in sandals. She didn't miss that feeling. She would always prefer the sand between her toes.

Londyn turned around, and Saylor stopped a considerable distance away. Her body was beautiful and slender and curvy — still in all of the right places. Saylor would never have known she was pregnant. Only her face was slightly fuller at this stage.

"Thank you for coming," Londyn smiled first, and Saylor could feel herself begin to relax a little.

"Welcome home, Londyn," Saylor wasn't quite sure what else to say, but she wanted to let her know how happy she was that they were going to have another baby. "I really am overjoyed for you and Nash. Your news… you're having another baby… that's so wonderful."

Londyn smiled wider. "It's such a miracle. I need this, Nash and I both do. No child will ever replace our Mia, but I feel as if she had a hand in sending this baby down to us. Her little brother or sister probably has already met her."

"I believe that too," Saylor spoke straight from her heart.

"I'm sure you're wondering why I wanted you here," Londyn broke the tension before it could have easily built up after they ceased the baby talk. Saylor waited. "See this tree…" Londyn turned around to face it again.

"The one that's weathered a few storms, even lightning, right?" Mia had told Saylor the stories through the years.

"Twice, actually. It's unexplainable how it's still standing, and strong. It's been hurt more than once. The kind of hurt that can knock you down and you'll never be the same.

If Things Were Different

Never recover. It's symbolic, Saylor. We've all hurt each other, but we've come out stronger and in healthier relationships than we had before." Londyn would never assume that Saylor and Max were strong if she had not heard it firsthand from Nash. The men had bonded again this morning, just as they always had in their years of friendship. And Max had brought up Saylor first. He wanted Nash to know that they too were solid together, like never before.

Saylor fought back the tears. What Londyn had said was simply beautiful. Without thinking, Saylor stood shoulder to shoulder with Londyn and she reached her arm around her back as they stared up at a tree that looked as if it could touch the heavens. What a comfort that tree was for so many reasons now.

"I'm going inside now," Londyn said to Saylor, "and I want you to talk to him."

Saylor felt her face flush. Londyn had set her up, she had pushed them together. Again.

"It's okay. Just get it out of the way. Nash was hesitant, too. Just do it. Find your peace. For this baby on the way." Saylor could not help it. Her mind immediately shifted to thoughts of — *here we go again! Do it for the baby. Make peace for the child Nash would have with another woman.*

When Londyn walked away, Saylor was afraid to turn around. She finally did though, and that's when she saw him halfway through the yard, moving slowly toward her. She froze inside. That man never changed. His swagger. His confidence. His beautiful face. And he now wore his hair shorter. He still looked both boyish and manly. That hadn't changed with the length of his hair. The sight of him would always give her the same feeling. And he would forever remain tucked inside the safest corner of her heart.

"My wife had this crazy idea that we are going to be able to get past the awkward," Nash said to her, and Saylor immediately grasped the fact that not once had Nash ever referred to Londyn as *his wife*. It was touching and it was territorial. She liked it more than she would have ever believed. The boundaries were back between them. The barrier was sturdy and sound. And it felt comfortable. Saylor was content on her side of the fence again.

"I think she may be right this time," Saylor replied, and Nash knew precisely what she had been referring to. The last time they were thrown together like this, Londyn believed the two of them belonged together. And that wasn't true, after all.

"I'm going to be a daddy again," Nash boasted, knowing that Saylor already knew.

She smiled wide at him. "I couldn't be happier for you and Londyn. I hope to meet her or him one day." Saylor wondered for the umpteenth time today, since she had heard the news, if she and her family would be a part of this baby's life just as they were with Mia's. She doubted that kind of closeness would be possible again. And that conclusion made her sad.

"I want this baby to heal your family, too," Nash said, acknowledging how they too had lost someone significant to all of them. Mia was truly vital to their family as well.

Saylor didn't fight the tears in her eyes this time. "I'd like that very much."

After a few moments of shared silence, Nash spoke again. "So are we good now? Did we get the awkward out of the way?"

Saylor laughed out loud at him. "Awkward has never existed between us."

"You're absolutely right," he said.

"And what we did was *right*, Nash," she emphasized, referring to everything that happened between them — from falling back into each other to saying goodbye again. She wanted him to know that she had survived a broken heart the second time around.

"On all accounts," Nash wholeheartedly agreed with her.

And Saylor finished his next thought, "No regrets."

Right or wrong, the two of them carried no remorse about anything throughout their short-lived time together, and especially now in their fulfilling lives apart.

About the author

From beginning to end, this book had my heart. I was captivated by the concept of what if things were different? I believe all of us have encountered something that happened (or did not happen) that had the power to change our lives. We can't help but imagine something being better, easier, or just altogether different than what we have. It's human nature. Sometimes it's about wanting what we don't have. Other times, it's a missed opportunity. Or maybe it's a burden we wish was lifted.

What I walked away with, after writing this story, was something so simple yet powerful. If, for whatever reason, we do not take the chance to see if something could be different — we have to open our eyes a little bit wider to appreciate the blessings already surrounding us. Choose to be happy. It's really that simple.

As always, thank you all for reading!

love,

Lori Bell